PENGUIN CLASSICS

THE LADIES OF THE CORRIDOR

DOROTHY PARKER—poet, short-story writer, critic, renowned wit, champion for social justice—was one of the unforgettable writers of her generation. Born August 22, 1893, she began her career at *Vogue* before joining the staff of *Vanity Fair,* where she later became its theater critic. In the 1920s she was a leading member of the Algonquin Round Table, the storied New York literary circle. Bestselling collections of her work include *Enough Rope* (1926), *Sunset Gun* (1928), *Laments for the Living* (1930), *Death and Taxes* (1931), and *The Portable Dorothy Parker* (1944). *The Ladies of the Corridor* was her final undertaking. She died on June 7, 1967, and is buried in Baltimore at the headquarters of her literary executor, the National Association for the Advancement of Colored People.

ARNAUD D'USSEAU was born on April 18, 1916, in Los Angeles, California. He was a notable playwright, screenwriter, and short-story writer. His works include *Tomorrow the World* (1943), *Deep Are the Roots* (1945), *Legend of Sarah* (1950), and, along with Dorothy Parker, *The Ladies in the Corridor* (1954), all of which were performed on Broadway. He died on January 29, 1990, in New York City.

MARION MEADE is both editor of *The Portable Dorothy Parker* and the author of *Dorothy Parker: What Fresh Hell Is This?* She has also written biographies of Woody Allen, Buster Keaton, Eleanor of Aquitaine, Madame Blavatsky, and Victoria Woodhull, as well as two novels about medieval France. Her most recent book is *Bobbed Hair and Bathtub Gin: Writers Running Wild in the Twenties*.

DOROTHY PARKER
AND ARNAUD
D'USSEAU

The Ladies of the Corridor

Introduction by MARION MEADE

PENGUIN BOOKS

PENGUIN BOOKS

Published by the Penguin Group

Penguin Group (USA) Inc., 375 Hudson Street, New York, New York 10014, U.S.A.

Penguin Group (Canada), 90 Eglinton Avenue East, Suite 700, Toronto,
Ontario, Canada M4P 2Y3 (a division of Pearson Penguin Canada Inc.)

Penguin Books Ltd, 80 Strand, London WC2R 0RL, England

Penguin Ireland, 25 St Stephen's Green, Dublin 2, Ireland (a division of Penguin Books Ltd)

Penguin Group (Australia), 250 Camberwell Road, Camberwell,
Victoria 3124, Australia (a division of Pearson Australia Group Pty Ltd)

Penguin Books India Pvt Ltd, 11 Community Centre, Panchsheel Park, New Delhi – 110 017, India

Penguin Group (NZ), 67 Apollo Drive, Rosedale, North Shore 0632,
New Zealand (a division of Pearson New Zealand Ltd)

Penguin Books (South Africa) (Pty) Ltd, 24 Sturdee Avenue, Rosebank,
Johannesburg 2196, South Africa

Penguin Books Ltd, Registered Offices:
80 Strand, London WC2R 0RL, England

First published in the United States of America by The Viking Press 1954
This edition with an introduction by Marion Meade published in Penguin Books 2008

ISBN 978-0-14-310531-2
CIP data available

Set in Sabon

To Susie

The ladies of the corridor
Find themselves involved, disgraced
Call witness to their principles
And deprecate the lack of taste.

—T. S. ELIOT, "SWEENEY ERECT"

Contents

Introduction

For all of her life, Dorothy Parker ate bacon raw because she never learned to cook. Neither did she dust, scrub, or pick up after herself. No matter, she didn't have to, because in the last century there existed the most extraordinary places to live: a clever combination of apartment, private house, and traditional hotel. These residence hotels could be found on the nicest streets in New York's most fashionable neighborhoods, and offered all the comforts of home plus a great deal more. No cooking, cleaning, or bed making; servants on call to do your bidding twenty-four hours a day. How often do you find a way to be treated like royalty?

Dorothy Parker was greatly enamored of residence hotels, which in their heyday catered to more or less permanent guests who rented by the month instead of the night, like regular hotels. Yes, she lived at certain periods of her life in Beverly Hills mansions, and she had also owned a 111-acre farm in Bucks County, Pennsylvania, but if left to her own devices she would check in to the first residence hotel she spotted. In the fall of 1952 she arrived in New York from Hollywood, having remarried and then separated from Alan Campbell, her second husband. Back in her beloved hometown, she was bubbling over with happiness: "I get up every morning and want to kiss the pavement," she announced.

Searching for a place to live, she discovered a small hotel on the Upper East Side that she thought would suit her nicely. At the Volney, located a few doors off Madison Avenue on Seventy-fourth Street, she rented a two-room apartment that boasted a decent-sized living room, small bedroom, and pantry with hot plate and mini-refrigerator. The hotel offered a restaurant and maid and laundry service, delivered her mail and *New York Times* to the door, took her phone messages; its doormen walked her poodle and whistled for taxis. The monthly rent of $275 ($2,500 today) was quite a lot in the 1950s, although not unreasonable for the location. A favorite of writers and theater people, the hotel was home to a mixture of professionals and retirees, men and women of all ages, married and single. Central Park was just down the street, the Metropolitan Museum of Art a few blocks north, and it was an easy walk to midtown.

Knowing about the Volney is important because the hotel would become both the inspiration and the backdrop for *The Ladies of the Corridor.*

For three decades Dorothy Parker had been a public figure. Beginning in the 1920s, as a founding member of the legendary Algonquin Round Table, she had acquired a reputation as one of the country's foremost humorists. During thirty years in the spotlight, she had poured out bestselling verse, short stories, and dramatic criticism, not to mention a string of Hollywood film scripts (including *A Star Is Born*). To her annoyance, however, she was perhaps best known as the mistress of the wisecrack, and her witty wasp-tongued quips were constantly being quoted—and misquoted. That was one side of Dorothy Parker, an amusing writer whom the public knew and loved. Another side, the private Parker, was a person whose lifelong struggles with depression and alcoholism had resulted in at least three suicide attempts. It was from the dark and violent side that *The Ladies of the Corridor* sprang.

Even though the play borrows a page from Parker's life it was a collaboration, and not her work alone. Throughout her writing career, she had been obliged to contend with an incurable handicap. Whereas she had no trouble composing lean verse and prose—some stories amounted to only a few pages—dialogue caused her to lose control. Plunging madly ahead, she would find herself with first acts the size of *War and Peace*. This was the reason her domestic comedy *Close Harmony* had been written with Elmer Rice, and all of her screenplays with her husband Alan Campbell. For structure and discipline, she needed a skilled writing partner. In Hollywood she had made the acquaintance of Arnaud d'Usseau, an engaging young fellow of thirty-six, whose then wife, Susan, a textile painter, had once operated the Book of the Day shop that stocked communist and left wing literature. Parker, who was a member of the Communist Party, moved in the same radical circles as the d'Usseaus. With playwright James Gow, d'Usseau had co-authored in the 1940s two Broadway productions, *Tomorrow the World* and *Deep Are the Roots*, propagandistic social dramas that had been commercial successes. Personally fond of d'Usseau, Parker decided she could team up with him. In 1952 they started discussing some of the special problems facing women in their forties and fifties. Together, they slowly shaped the material into a meditation on the waste of human lives.

The Ladies of the Corridor is a searing real-life drama about women living on their own in a New York residence hotel. The characters are empty nesters struggling with lives that have lost their centers. Husbands are dead. Children, if any, are married and raising families, with less time for aging parents. Like generations of women before them, these are the people who had never worked outside their homes, and now find themselves permanently laid off from their professions of wife, mother, and housekeeper. They fill idle hours with movies, mystery novels, endless needlepoint, and restorative naps.

The main character is Lulu Ames, a stylish young widow from Akron, who arrives at the Hotel Marlowe with her hatboxes and a miniature French poodle in the hope of making up for years lost in a suffocating marriage. Soon she falls in love with Paul Osgood, the divorced owner of a local bookshop and an attractive thirty-eight-year-old who is a dozen years her junior. (Parker herself enjoyed flings with younger men.) Bleaching her hair, she begins to fantasize about a permanent relationship. Without rescue by a fairy-tale prince, she faces the alternative of a desolate life, just like the women she passes in the hotel lobby. Their lives, a daily reminder of the crushing reality of having nothing whatsoever to do, depress her and she vows never to become one of them.

If Lulu is the kind of sweet, dreamy woman that audiences would root for, another leading character is a monster: Grace Nichols. Confined to a wheelchair, she uses blackmail to imprison her adult homosexual son. Two additional characters could not be more different. Mildred Tynan is a young divorcee who, after fleeing her fearsome marriage to a sado-masochist, is now wrestling with alcoholism. Dependent on alimony checks and without job skills to support herself, she begins to crumble. Contrastingly, Constance Mercer is a hard-working widow who has succeeded in engineering a business career for herself.

In the Marlowe lobby, where the ever-present vase of salmon-pink gladioli is never allowed to wilt, sits a kind of Greek chorus, a pair of women who remind Mildred Tynan of vegetables "sitting there in their bins, waiting for the garbage collector." She accuses Mrs. Gordon and Mrs. Lauterbach of being "old hags in the corridor."

The play took about a year to complete, with most of the writing done in Arnaud d'Usseau's apartment in the East Fifties. His wife was a terrific cook, "so Dorothy came around for a lot of free meals," he recalled. It was he who came up with the title *The Ladies of the Corridor*, taking a line from T. S. Eliot's 1920 poem "Sweeney Erect."

Luckily, there was no problem obtaining a first-class Broadway production, because any work by Parker, even one whose main point was the oppression of women, was bound to be an anticipated event. It was quickly optioned by Walter Fried, a major league producer of such plays as Arthur Miller's *Death of a Salesman* and *All My Sons*. The powerhouse director was Harold Clurman, who after cutting his teeth with

The Group Theater in the 1930s had recently staged hits like *The Member of the Wedding* and *Desire Under the Elms*. As part of his cast of Broadway veterans, Clurman chose for the role of Lulu's Paul Osgood an interesting newcomer, Walter Matthau, who would of course go on to become one of Hollywood's biggest stars.

"The first day of rehearsal," Clurman remembered, "when we actually put the play on the stage and it was working out very nicely, [Parker] began to cry because there it was coming to life." In truth, the look and feel of the play thrilled her. Sometimes she sniffled, and sometimes tears ran down her cheeks. So much of it was autobiographical; almost every female character had roots in her own history or the experiences of people she knew. The scary wheelchair mother, for instance, was a delicate composite of her own mother-in-law and one of her very dearest friends. As rehearsals continued, everything Parker did began to irritate Clurman, who was in the driver's seat and determined to get on with the business at hand. With no time for crocodile tears, he tried to ignore her. If she balked at giving him credit for knowing audiences, he refused to acknowledge her considerable experience in theater and film as a drama critic and author of a Broadway comedy, in addition to dozens of screenplays. So when he suggested cutting Mildred's suicide, Parker shrugged off his advice. With the friction mounting, they practically came to blows over the ending.

By the final scene, after the affair with Paul has not worked out, Lulu reluctantly considers attending a movie with Mesdames Gordon, Lauterbach, and Nichols.

MRS. GORDON: Now what are you gonna do? Sit in your room and do your needlepoint all day?

MRS. LAUTERBACH: Oh, you don't want to do that.

MRS. GORDON: I bought an extra ticket yesterday for Mrs. Nichols.

MRS. LAUTERBACH: But we can always get another for her.

LULU: Well. . . .

MRS. LAUTERBACH: Something to take your mind off your
   troubles.

LULU: All right.

MRS. LAUTERBACH: Wonderful!

MRS. GORDON: We'll meet you in the lobby at three o'clock.

It was Parker's belief that Lulu was trapped. But Clurman objected to her becoming one of the ladies of the
corridor. The play needed an upbeat finale. Parker, uncon-
vinced, simply could not tolerate happy endings and, not
one to mince words, had once engaged in a futile argument
with the film producer Samuel Goldwyn, insisting that
"in all history, which has held billions and billions of human beings, not a single one ever had a happy ending."
Clurman, however, insisted there must be an appropriate
payoff, just as theatergoers needed somebody to pull for.
Those upset by Mildred's suicide might be frightened by
Lulu's failure to find even a tiny ray of hope. Trust him,
Clurman told the writers, because he knew best. The ending had to go.

   Under the circumstances, the protesting Parker and d'Usseau
had little choice but to write an optimistic replacement. While
only a few lines were actually changed, the meaning of the
play became completely different. The new scene shows Lulu
exchanging greetings with Mrs. Gordon and Mrs. Lauterbach
in the corridor while they are collecting their newspapers and
planning their day. When the two of them ask her to a movie,
she politely says no thanks.

   Mrs. Gordon tells her: "Mustn't let yourself get lonely."

   As she heads to the elevator, Lulu insists that she is fine. "I'm
not even scared. You see, I've learned from looking around,
there is something worse than loneliness—and that's the fear
of it. I hope the movie is good."

   The Ladies of the Corridor opened on October 21, 1953.
In a panic, Parker decided that she was not going to attend the
premiere. In the end, however, she sat through the performance

like a condemned prisoner on death row. Later there followed a cast party and the usual first-night ritual of waiting for the reviews. Accompanied by Arnaud and Susan d'Usseau, and by Kate Harkin Mostel, who played the small part of the chambermaid and who in private life was the wife of the actor Zero Mostel, she found herself surrounded by close friends. For the next several hours, she kept busy biting her nails and drinking scotch. After midnight somebody went to an all-night newsstand and fetched the early editions of the morning papers.

Kate Mostel remembered that the reviews were disappointing, "not rotten, but not good." For any play, the most crucial notice appeared in the *New York Times*. Giving *The Ladies of the Corridor* a cool reception, admittedly bored, critic Brooks Atkinson thought Parker and d'Usseau had gone to "considerable trouble to reiterate the obvious," which was that older women are "pathetic and lonely creatures." He didn't need to attend the theater to be reminded. Worst of all, Atkinson slammed the play for containing more hackneyed ideas than he would have expected from artists the caliber of Parker and d'Usseau.

Once the *Times* review was known, Parker tried to make a graceful exit. Pulling on her coat, she joked, "Does anybody need a lady pool shark?" Atkinson's belittling remarks, however, were truly devastating to her.

In spite of the dismissive *Times* review, five of the eight New York papers responded approvingly. One of the play's biggest admirers was George Jean Nathan, the venerable dean of New York drama critics writing in the *Journal-American*, who praised *The Ladies of the Corridor* as "completely honest." During balloting of the Drama Critics Circle in the spring, he would vote for *The Ladies of the Corridor* as the best play of the 1953–1954 season. That was the good news; the not so good news was the play was dead and buried by then, having closed the week of Thanksgiving after forty-five performances. What happened? Could women's issues be the kiss of death? Was the work too radical, too depressing? It offered wit and laughter, even sexual passion, but still failed to attract an audience.

Two years later, Parker sounded remarkably cheerful about the experience. "Writing that play was the best time I ever had," she told an interviewer from *The Paris Review*. Indeed, she would go so far as to say it was "the only thing I have ever done in which I had great pride." And after all, the critics had not really burned her at the stake.

Others associated with the production failed to muster the same enthusiasm. Parker may have been "a very funny lady," Harold Clurman allowed, but he happened to find her "a very sad person," a "bleeding heart liberal" with a talent for melodrama. In the eyes of producer Walter Fried, the play should never have been performed. It bombed, he said, because it was not strictly a play. It was an assortment of unrelated episodes lacking dramatic unity, which "read much better than it could possibly play."

Off and on for the last twenty-five years of her life, not including a three-year stint in Hollywood, Parker would continue to make her home at the Volney. But affection for the hotel never prevented her from ridiculing it every chance she got. For that matter, the Volney sparked some of her most ghoulish mockery. Talking to her buddy Quentin Reynolds, a journalist also living there, she mentioned a problem. Had he noticed the number of older residents? And what about the elevator? It reminded her of a telephone booth. Think what might happen if any of the old folks—she was really thinking of herself—died in their suites? Could the undertaker safely arrange their removal? The passenger elevator could not accommodate a gurney unless it was carried out standing, and the service elevator was used for collecting trash.

The solution, she told Reynolds, was for the Volney to construct a chute between one of its upper floors and the Frank Campbell Funeral Home located several blocks up Madison Avenue. She could just picture the scene. "We'd arrive in good condition and the trip would take a minute," she said. At that point, with years and years left to live, Parker got a big kick from those types of grim jokes.

On a fine June afternoon in 1967, Dorothy Parker died of a heart attack in apartment 6F. Discovered by a chambermaid, her body was delivered to the Campbell Funeral Home. Not by chute of course.

Half a century after the original production, *The Ladies of the Corridor* was revived by the Peccadillo Theatre Company in a wonderful off-Broadway production that restored the original ending and got magnificent reviews. "As unyielding and coruscating a portrait of women before feminism as I have ever seen," reported Honor Moore in the *New York Times.* Nobody had to tell post–women's liberation audiences what the play was about—themselves, their mothers, their mother-in-laws. Everybody got it, even though by this time the Hotel Marlowe "ladies" had mostly become clichés, as historical as Scarlett O'Hara's corsets. For one thing, women in 2005 thought of themselves not as ladies but as women, and for another, they frequently kept their own names after marriage. Savvy women in their fifties and sixties had better things to do than idle in hotel lobbies with mystery novels. Usually they were too busy holding down jobs, running to the gym, or—the weekend warriors—training for marathons. They got hip and knee replacements, and dated (well, occasionally) thirty-eight-year-old men. And while needlepoint remained popular, it was by no means their main activity. Individuals like Mrs. Gordon and Mrs. Lauterbach seemed to be extinct, and the era of residence hotels had also vanished and seemed unlikely to return.

If you ever find yourself strolling in the city near Central Park, turn down Seventy-fourth Street and walk along the peaceful block between Fifth and Madison. At No. 23 is an Italian Renaissance palazzo-style building with a smart gray canopy. No longer a hotel, the Volney has been overhauled into a fifteen-story cooperative apartment house where a one-bedroom unit is priced about $900,000. In Manhattan's tight real estate market, inventive ideas are needed. To accommodate families, residents have been obliged to knock down walls and combine small apartments. Unusual items, such as strollers, have been known to appear in the Volney elevator. Dorothy Parker's ladies of the corridor would not easily recognize the building they called home.

MARION MEADE

NOTES

xi *"I get up"*   Marion Meade, *What Fresh Hell Is This?* (Villard, 1988), 346, quoting *New York World Telegram and Sun*.

xi *Searching for a place*   According to friends, Parker may have tested several residence hotels before settling on the Volney.

xiii *This was the reason*   All five of Dorothy Parker's plays were collaborations: *Close Harmony* (with Elmer Rice, 1924), *The Happiest Man* (with Alan Campbell, 1939, never produced), *The Coast of Illyria* (with Ross Evans, 1949, Margo Jones Repertory Theatre, Dallas), *The Ladies of the Corridor* (with Arnaud d'Usseau, 1953), and *The Ice Age* (with Arnaud d'Usseau, 1955, never produced). Her most distinguished collaborator was Rice, author of *The Adding Machine* and the Pulitzer Prize–winning *Street Scene*.

xiv *"sitting there in their bins"*   *The Ladies of the Corridor*, Dorothy Parker and Arnaud d'Usseau (Viking Press, 1954), 112.

xiv *"old hags"*   Ibid.

xiv *"so Dorothy came around"*   Arnaud d'Usseau interview with Louise Lieberman, 1989, courtesy of Marie-Christine d'Usseau.

xiv *first-class Broadway production*   In addition to *Death of a Salesman* and *All My Sons* (Arthur Miller), Walter Fried also produced *The Time of the Cuckoo* (Arthur Laurents). Harold Clurman directed Clifford Odets's *Awake and Sing!* and *Golden Boy* for the Group Theater, as well as *The Member of the Wedding* (Carson McCullers).

xv *"The first day"*   Harold Clurman interview (1979), Columbia University Oral History Research Office.

xv *"Now what"   The Ladies of the Corridor*, 72. From Peccadillo Theatre Company's 2005 script, revised and edited by Dan Wackerman. As no copies of the discarded Parker-d'Usseau script survived, director Wackerman reconstructed the ending out of available source materials including reviews of the original production and discussions with a Parker scholar. The accuracy of the reproduction was authenticated by the d'Usseau family.

xvi *"in all history"*   Garson Kanin, *Hollywood* (Viking Press, 1974) , 284.

xvi *"mustn't let yourself"   The Ladies of the Corridor*, 120.

xvi *"not even scared"*   Ibid.

xvii *"not rotten"*   Kate Mostel and Madeline Gilford, *170 Years of Show Business* (Random House, 1978), 130.

xvii *"considerable trouble"   New York Times,* Oct. 22, 1953.

xvii *"completely honest"   New York Journal-American,* Apr. 4, 1954.

xviii *"Writing that play"*   Dorothy Parker interview, *The Paris Review*, "Writers at Work," 1956; reprinted in *The Portable Dorothy Parker* (Penguin, 2006), 580.

xviii *"the only thing"*   Ibid.

xviii *"a very funny lady"   Los Angeles Times,* Nov. 29, 1970.

xviii *"bleeding heart liberal"*   Harold Clurman interview (1979), Columbia University Oral History Research Office.

xviii *"read much better"*   John Keats, *You Might As Well Live* (Simon and Schuster, 1970), 264.

xviii *"We'd arrive"* Quentin Reynolds, *By Quentin Reynolds* (McGraw-Hill, 1963), 6.

xix *"as unyielding"* *New York Times,* Sept. 16, 2005.

xix *Volney . . . cooperative* Coco Pazzo, an expensive Italian restaurant, now shares the same address.

Suggestions for Further Reading and Listening

Calhoun, Randall. *Dorothy Parker: A Bio-Bibliography*. Westport, CT: Greenwood Press, 1993.

Cooper, Wyatt. "Whatever You Think Dorothy Parker Was Like, She Wasn't," *Esquire*, July 1968 (56–57, 61, 110–114).

Drennan, Robert, Ed. *The Algonquin Wits*. New York: Citadel Press, 1968.

Fitzpatrick, Kevin C. *A Journey into Dorothy Parker's New York*. Berkeley, CA: Roaring Forties Press, 2005.

Frewin, Leslie. *The Late Mrs. Dorothy Parker*. New York: Macmillan, 1986.

Gaines, James R. *Wit's End: Days and Nights of the Algonquin Round Table*. New York: Harcourt Brace Jovanovich, 1977.

Harriman, Margaret Case. *The Vicious Circle: The Story of the Algonquin Round Table*. New York: Rinehart, 1951.

Keats, John. *You Might As Well Live: The Life and Times of Dorothy Parker*. New York: Simon and Schuster, 1970.

Kinney, Arthur F. *Dorothy Parker, Revised*. New York: Twayne, 1998.

Meade, Marion. *Dorothy Parker: What Fresh Hell Is This?* New York: Penguin, 2007.

———. *Bobbed Hair and Bathtub Gin: Writers Running Wild in the Twenties*. New York: Nan A. Talese/Doubleday, 2004. Harvest Books, 2005.

Melzer, Sondra. *The Rhetoric of Rage: Women in Dorothy Parker*. New York: Peter Lang Publishing Co., 2001.

Mostel, Kate Harkin, and Madeline Gilford. *170 Years of Show Business*. New York: Random House, 1978.

Parker, Dorothy. *The Portable Dorothy Parker*. Penguin Classics Deluxe Edition. Ed. Marion Meade. New York: Penguin, 2006.

———. *The Paris Review Interviews I*: Intro. Philip Gourevitch. New York: Picador, 2006.

———. *The Poetry and Short Stories of Dorothy Parker*. New York: Random House (Modern Library), 1994.

———. *Complete Stories*. Intro. Regina Barreca. New York: Penguin, 2002.

———. *American Poetry: The Twentieth Century, Volume I: Henry Adams to Dorothy Parker*. New York: Library of America, 2000.

———. www.dorothyparker.com. (Dorothy Parker Web site)

Perelman, S. J. *The Last Laugh*. New York: Simon and Schuster, 1981.

Pettit, Rhonda S. *A Gendered Collision: Sentimentalism and Modernism in Dorothy Parker's Poetry and Fiction*. Madison, NJ: Farleigh Dickinson University Press, 2000.

——— (Ed.) *The Critical Waltz: Essays on the Work of Dorothy Parker*. Madison, NJ: Fairleigh Dickinson University Press, 2005.

Thurber, James. *The Years With Ross*. Boston: Little Brown, 1959.

White, E. B. *Here Is New York*. Intro. Roger Angell. New York: The Little Bookroom, 2000.

Yagoda, Ben. *About Town: The New Yorker and the World It Made*. New York: Scribner, 2000.

AUDIO AND DVD

Bobbed Hair and Bathtub Gin: Writers Running Wild in the Twenties. Blackstone Audiobooks, 2004. Read by Lorna Raver.

The Complete New Yorker: Eighty Years of the Nation's Greatest Magazine. Ed. David Remnick. New York: The New Yorker, 2005 (hardcover book; 8 DVD-Roms).

The Dorothy Parker Audio Collection. HarperAudio (abridged edition), 2004. Read by Christine Baranski, Cynthia Nixon, Alfre Woodard, and Shirley Booth.

Dorothy Parker: What Fresh Hell Is This? Blackstone Audiobooks, 1997. Read by Grace Conlin.

Essential Parker. Caedmon/HarperAudio, 2006. Read by Christine Baranski and Cynthia Nixon.

Selected Readings from The Portable Dorothy Parker. Blackstone Audiobooks (abridged edition), 2007. Read by Lorna Raver.

Voice of the Poets, American Wits: Ogden Nash, Dorothy Parker, Phyllis McGinley. Random House Audio, 2003.

The Ladies of the Corridor

The Ladies of the Corridor was first presented by Walter Fried at the Longacre Theatre, New York, on October 21, 1953, with the following cast.

The Characters (in order of their appearance)

MRS. GORDON: JUNE WALKER
MR. HUMPHRIES: ROBERT VAN HOOTON
MRS. LAUTERBACH: VERA ALLEN
MRS. NICHOLS: FRANCES STARR
HARRY: LONNY CHAPMAN
CASEY: LOUIS CRISS
LULU AMES: EDNA BEST
SASSY: TASSLE
MILDRED TYNAN: BETTY FIELD
ROBERT AMES: CLEMENT BRACE
BETSY AMES: CAROL WHEELER
CONSTANCE MERCER: MARGARET BARKER
IRMA: KATE HARKIN
PAUL OSGOOD: WALTER MATTHAU
TOM LINSCOTT: DONALD MCKEE
MARY LINSCOTT: HARRIETT MACGIBBON

Staged by HAROLD CLURMAN
Settings by RALPH ALSWANG
Costumes by NOEL TAYLOR

The action of the play takes place during a year in the Hotel Marlowe in the East Sixties in New York City.

ACT ONE

ACT ONE

SCENE ONE

The scene is the Hotel Marlowe in the East Sixties in New York City. The time is a late afternoon in November.

The Marlowe is an old hotel with an atmosphere that suggests another and more opulent era. It is not shabby, it is efficiently managed, but there has been no attempt to modernize its decorations, which are considered part of its charm. It has but few transient guests and no commercial trade. Occasionally a married couple is found living there, and sometimes a bachelor, but most of the suites and single rooms are occupied by ladies alone. Mostly they are widows (there are seven and a half million widows in the United States); some less fortunate are divorced; and there's an infrequent nondescript who is only separated.

The action of the play begins in the lobby, which is small and only a part of which we see. There is a counter which serves as a desk, and behind it the rows of pigeonholes for the mail. Also back of the counter, barely visible, is a switchboard.

Opposite the counter is a group composed of a sofa and a brass ashtray on a long brass leg; and against the wall, back of this, is a commode bearing a vase filled with those salmon-pink gladioli which are peculiar to hotels. The door to the street and the passage to the elevators are invisible to the audience. However, they are both in full view of those who sit on the sofa, which is why they sit there.

When the curtain rises, we discover Mr. Humphries, the hotel manager, mild, dapper, and eager to please, behind the desk. He is listening politely to Maude Gordon. She is a small woman admitting to sixty, who frequently has been compared to Dresden china. Her short-cut hair is sedulously curled and tinted gentian blue. She wears a dark-blue dress with white collar and cuffs, and a tiny hat. Over an arm she carries a mink cape by which she recognizes the autumn. Mrs. Lauterbach, another widow, is seated erectly on the sofa. She is rather bigger than Mrs. Gordon and several years younger. She too wears a dark-blue dress with white collar and cuffs, and a small black hat with a veil reaching to the end of her nose. Her mink cape is over the arm of the sofa, and in her lap is a lending-library book in a cellophane dust jacket.

MRS. GORDON (*in a high voice and with an extravagant Southern accent*): It's a vile thing, real disgraceful! Happening in an exclusive hotel like this, being a guest here ten years ago last March, be eleven years this coming March!

MR. HUMPHRIES: I'm sorry, Mrs. Gordon. The cashier is out now, but as soon as he comes back, I'll—

MRS. GORDON: I don't care to deal with any hirelings, Mr. Humphries! I'm not one to make complaints, but when I do I believe in going right to the top! Look at that bill! Charging me with telephone calls the tenth, eleventh, and twelfth! Why, I never picked the telephone up in all those days!

MR. HUMPHRIES: Please don't worry, Mrs. Gordon. We'll straighten it out.

MRS. GORDON: I'm not doing any worrying, Mr. Humphries! I don't have to! My conscience is perfectly clear. Now you just take that pen of yours and write down the word "mistake" and show it to that shiftless little old cashier you got!

MR. HUMPHRIES: That really isn't necessary.

MRS. GORDON: You go ahead and do what I tell you! (*As if*

humoring a child, Mr. Humphries does as Mrs. Gordon demands.) That's better. (*Then, with a smile*) Thank you, Mr. Humphries. You're always so sweet about everything. (*She turns and goes to where Mrs. Lauterbach is seated on the sofa.*)

MRS. LAUTERBACH: Greetings, fair lady. Sit ye doon. (*Mrs. Gordon sits down, puts her cape over the arm of the sofa.*) You've been having a little trouble?

MRS. GORDON: Nothing I hate like a fuss—but a lady alone, it seems like everybody's out to cheat her. Well, what's new on the Rialto?

MRS. LAUTERBACH: I see you changed the polish on your nails. That's a nice becoming color. What else you been doing?

MRS. GORDON: What a day! I'm just about wore out. Had my polish changed; had my hair done; took those shoes back that were killing me. That little old clerk, selling me shoes a size too small! I told him my feet are small enough as they are; always had compliments on my little feet. How do you like my hair?

MRS. LAUTERBACH: Lovely. I can't wait for mine to go gray so I can have it made blue.

MRS. GORDON (*complacently patting her hair*): Well, it's a trouble and it's an expense, but it's real enjoyable. (*Noting a letter in Mrs. Lauterbach's hand*) Oh—you been upstairs writing letters?

MRS. LAUTERBACH: Just this one to my daughter.

MRS. GORDON: Why don't you mail it? You got a stamp on it.

MRS. LAUTERBACH (*diffidently*): I wrote asking if I could come up to Oswego to see them over Thanksgiving. Now I'm kind of scared. I think I'll wait for the morning mail, because there might be a letter from them asking me to come. If this got there first, it'd make me look pushing.

MRS. GORDON: Your grandchildren all right? They seem to ail so much of the time.

MRS. LAUTERBACH (*hurt*): Oh, no, they don't, Mrs. Gordon. They're beautiful, healthy kiddies. Oh, the measles last summer when I thought I was going up there—but you got to expect those things with children.

MRS. GORDON: Well, I never had any children, so I never expected anything.

Mrs. Nichols and her son enter from the direction of the elevators. Mrs. Nichols, an arthritic, is confined to a wheelchair—not an old-fashioned cumbersome one, but a low, lightweight aluminum model such as paraplegics use. Despite her ailment, Mrs. Nichols is all elegance. She is dressed softly and beautifully. From the perfect hat set so carefully on her perfect hair to the pretty little feet partly covered by a light afghan, she is all expense, taste, and femininity. Charles Nichols pushes the chair. He is tall, lean, finely drawn. Look carefully at him, and he is beautiful. But he should have been handsome at first sight.

MRS. LAUTERBACH (*gaily*): Well, here's our third Musketeer. Greetings, fair lady. Sit ye doon. (*Catching herself*) Er—come over here with us, Mrs. Nichols.

MRS. GORDON: Good afternoon, Charlie.

CHARLES: Good afternoon, ladies. (*He pushes the wheelchair next to the sofa, begins tucking the afghan around Mrs. Nichols' knees.*) That too tight?

MRS. NICHOLS: That's very nice, dear. Now go along for your walk. Mustn't keep your friends the animals waiting.

MRS. LAUTERBACH: Off to the zoo again, Charlie?

MRS. NICHOLS: Oh, he wouldn't miss a day. Really, I believe he knows every one of those animals by name. There's Rosie, the hippopotamus—and Chiang, the elephant. (*To Charles*) Charles, tell them about Chiang.

CHARLES: There's nothing much to tell, Grace. She's just a nice old lady with a man's name.

MRS. GORDON: Well, give her our love.

CHARLES: I'll be back soon, Grace. Good-by for the present, ladies. (*He goes toward the street entrance, disappears.*)

MRS. GORDON: Isn't that sweet, the way he calls you by your first name? Why, I never think of you as mother and son.

MRS. LAUTERBACH: You two are just like brother and sister.

MRS. NICHOLS: So many people are kind enough to say that. I can't help taking it as a compliment.

MRS. LAUTERBACH: I never saw anything prettier than his devotion to you. I wish mine would be a little more— (*Catches herself.*)

MRS. NICHOLS: I've always tried to help the boy forget that he never knew his father. His poor father—just a month to the day, before Charlie was born—(*The ladies shake their heads sympathetically. Mrs. Nichols determinedly changes the subject.*) I suppose you two have been your usual busy selves. (*To Mrs. Gordon*) I see you had the polish on your nails changed.

MRS. GORDON: Yes, Rosy Garter. Do you like it? Don't make my hand look too stumpy, does it?

MRS. NICHOLS: Oh, no. Delightful.

MRS. GORDON: Look, you ladies want to see something? (*She takes a thimble from her handbag.*)

MRS. LAUTERBACH: Isn't that cunning? You see it, Mrs. Nichols. A red, white, and blue thimble.

MRS. GORDON: I was in the five-and-ten. There was this whole counter of them—well, they'll never miss this one.

MRS. LAUTERBACH: Virginia Gordon, you're a holy terror. Isn't she, Mrs. Nichols?

MRS. NICHOLS (*indulgently*): She certainly is.

MRS. LAUTERBACH: Last week it was that little pink comb. What do you want a red, white, and blue thimble for?

MRS. GORDON: Oh, I don't know. It's just fun to do it.

Mrs. Gordon puts the thimble into her handbag. There is a stir behind the desk.

MR. HUMPHRIES: Harry! Front!

Harry appears from the direction of the elevators, goes toward the front door. Harry is twenty-seven, dark, well built, admirably coordinated. His uniform is a single-breasted green suit with brass buttons and the initial M embroidered in gold on the collar; it is livery, not costume, and he wears it with style.

HARRY (*as he crosses, calling back over his shoulder*): Casey, you want to give me a hand with these bags?

He goes out as Casey comes from the direction of the elevators. Casey is a nice-looking boy of nineteen or twenty; he does not wear his uniform with anywhere near Harry's smartness and confidence. As he crosses and goes out, the three ladies turn as one, and watch to see what is going to happen.

MRS. LAUTERBACH: It's a lady all by herself.
MRS. NICHOLS: Look at all that baggage. Two hatboxes— and what's that square one? A shoebox?
MRS. GORDON: Those kind of things are nothing but an expense. Just means another tip to the porter.
MRS. LAUTERBACH: What's that coat? Broadtail?
MRS. GORDON: Won't wear.
MRS. NICHOLS: No warmth to it.

During the preceding speeches Casey has returned, carrying two suitcases; he goes out toward the elevator. Harry follows him, carrying various pieces of luggage. Now Lulu Ames enters. She actually is in her early fifties, but she might be ten years younger. She is tall, slender, and elegant, and is dressed all in black, even to her gloves and her stockings. The effect is one of deep mourning, though she wears neither crape nor enshrouding veils. She carries a miniature French poodle, smartly clipped. As she goes toward the desk the ladies watch her.

LULU: I'm Mrs. Elliott Ames. I hope you got my wire.

MR. HUMPHRIES (*handing her a pen*): Yes, indeed, Mrs. Ames. Will you register? (*As Lulu registers*) Did you have a pleasant journey?

LULU: Very nice, thank you.

MR. HUMPHRIES: A charming little dog you have. A real beauty, isn't he?

LULU: Yes, she is, isn't she? Oh, I'm expecting my son and his wife. When they come will you please send them right up?

MR. HUMPHRIES: Your suite is ready, and I hope you'll find it quite comfortable. (*He comes out from behind the desk; goes with Lulu toward the elevators.*) If there's anything we can do to make you feel at home, why just let us—

They are out, and we do not hear the rest of Mr. Humphries' speech.

MRS. GORDON: Royalty has come to the Hotel Marlowe.

MRS. LAUTERBACH: Girls, do you think both these clips in my hat are too much? Tell me honestly.

MRS. NICHOLS: What did she say her name was?

MRS. GORDON: I'll tell you. (*She rises, goes to the desk, and looks at the register.*)

MRS. LAUTERBACH (*as Mrs. Gordon crosses*): That Mrs. Gordon, isn't she terrible?

MRS. GORDON (*to the others, in a piercing whisper*): Mrs. Elliott Ames, Akron, Ohio. Two l's and two t's in Elliott.

MRS. NICHOLS: They couldn't do much more with it.

MRS. GORDON (*returning to the sofa*): She's got Ten-Sixteen.

MRS. LAUTERBACH: On our corridor.

MRS. NICHOLS: Well, friend or foe, we'll soon know.

MRS. LAUTERBACH: A cute little dog she's got.

MRS. GORDON: I hope it isn't one of those yapping kind. I like a big hunting dog myself. Kind we always have down in Virginia.

MRS. LAUTERBACH: A dog's a great comfort in a bereavement.

MRS. NICHOLS: I suppose a widow, poor thing.

MRS. GORDON: All widows aren't to be pitied. Of course, it's kind of hard at first. I know; I went through it twice when my dear ones passed on. Well, there's no use crying over spilt milk. (*Mr. Humphries returns from the direction of the elevator. Mrs. Gordon calls to him.*) By the day or by the week, Mr. Humphries?

MR. HUMPHRIES: I beg pardon, Mrs. Gordon?

MRS. GORDON: Our new guest. By the day or by the week?

MR. HUMPHRIES: Mrs. Ames has taken a suite by the month. (*He goes behind the desk.*)

MRS. GORDON: Well, ladies, what's on the carpet for tonight?

MRS. LAUTERBACH: Right now I've got to take my book back.

MRS. NICHOLS: That book any good?

MRS. LAUTERBACH: *Murder in a Gilded Cage.* I got all the way up to page two hundred and eight before I remembered I'd read it before.

MRS. GORDON: Tell them you won't pay for it. They ought to keep better track. Mrs. Nichols, you feel up to taking in a movie tonight?

MRS. NICHOLS: Oh, I don't know. Maybe you ladies better run along without me. I'm such an old nuisance.

MRS. LAUTERBACH: Why, I never heard such talk. You a nuisance!

MRS. NICHOLS: I'm so conspicuous in this awful thing.

MRS. GORDON: I wish I could be that kind of conspicuous. Why, when you come rolling into the movie house with Charlie pushing you, that chair's like a queen's chariot. I declare, you're positively regal.

MRS. NICHOLS: Well, if you really want me—

MRS. LAUTERBACH (*rising*): Good. Now we all got a nice busy evening ahead. See you girls later. (*She goes toward the street entrance.*)

MRS. GORDON (*when Mrs. Lauterbach has gone*): Looks to me like Mrs. Lauterbach is putting on weight. I almost said something to her about it.

Harry appears, takes his position by the desk. At the same time Mrs. Gordon rises.

MRS. GORDON: Well, I got to get my beauty nap. You know me: every day of my life I take off all my clothes and go to bed for one hour. Best thing in the world for the complexion. Don't do you a bit of good unless you take off every stitch.

MRS. NICHOLS: Now, if you're going up, I'm going up too. I'm not going to sit alone with everybody staring at me.

MRS. GORDON: I'll give you a little ride to the elevator.

HARRY (*crossing to Mrs. Nichols' wheelchair*): Let me do that for you, Mrs. Gordon.

MRS. GORDON: Why, that's real sweet of you, Harry. Always so obliging.

MRS. NICHOLS: I don't know what the ladies in the Marlowe would do without Harry.

The three go in the direction of the elevators, and for a moment the lobby is empty save for Mr. Humphries, who is putting envelopes into the pigeonholes. His back is turned when Mildred Tynan enters from the direction of the street. Mildred is perhaps thirty-five; she is small and delicately made, and she must have been an extraordinarily pretty girl. Now there are a strain and an apprehension about her, but she keeps a curiously touching charm that should have somebody to protect it. She wears a brown polo coat and is hatless. She carries a handbag and a brown paper sack unmistakably enclosing a bottle of whisky. She looks quickly at Mr. Humphries and tries to get to the elevators while his back is turned. She does not succeed.

MR. HUMPHRIES (*turning*): Oh, Mrs. Tynan, may I speak to you for a moment? (*He comes out from behind the desk.*)

MILDRED: Oh, darn you, Mr. Humphries. I thought I could get past without your seeing me.

MR. HUMPHRIES: I hate to bother you, Mrs. Tynan, but if you could let us have a little something on your bill.

MILDRED: It isn't that I don't want to, Mr. Humphries. I feel simply awful about it. It's just that my check hasn't come yet. It should have been here the first of last week.

MR. HUMPHRIES: Please understand, I'm not saying this for myself, but the owners are after me pretty hard—

MILDRED: Mail from California—sometimes it gets delayed. Hasn't that ever happened to you?

MR. HUMPHRIES: I suppose it does happen, but when yours is delayed so many times—

MILDRED (*in a sudden outburst*): Don't I know it! It's late every month, and not by accident either! It's just another way to humiliate me! (*Then, recovering*) I'm sorry. You know as soon as my check comes I'll pay all I can on my bill.

MR. HUMPHRIES: If there was only some way you could hurry it up.

MILDRED: Got any suggestions?

MR. HUMPHRIES. Please, Mrs. Tynan. You see, there's a long waiting list, and, as the owners point out, we could use your room most advantageously for transient guests.

MILDRED: Yes, I know.

MR. HUMPHRIES: And they keep bringing to my attention that you haven't been using the restaurant. As you know, a hotel cannot exist on its rooms alone.

MILDRED: Yes, I know. Look, Mr. Humphries, if the check isn't here soon I'll telephone my husband's lawyer and tell him that something must be done immediately.

MR. HUMPHRIES: I wish you would.

MILDRED: Well, it's been nice talking, but there isn't anything more to say, is there?

MR. HUMPHRIES: I'm afraid there is, Mrs. Tynan. There have been several complaints recently.

MILDRED (*defiantly*): About what, for heaven's sake?

MR. HUMPHRIES: Well—about this. (*He indicates the brown paper sack.*)

MILDRED: Oh. But I never go out of my own room.

MR. HUMPHRIES: Well, they say—it seems you're rather fond of singing. Sometimes it is a little—if you could keep it softer.

MILDRED: Ah, now, really, Mr. Humphries! All right, they win. Tell the dear ladies I'll keep it down.

MR. HUMPHRIES: I was sure you'd cooperate. And please understand—this matter of the bill—I intensely dislike bringing it up again. It's simply the position I'm in.

MILDRED: And please understand, I intensely dislike owing my bill. It's simply the position *I'm* in.

MR. HUMPHRIES: Well, thank you, Mrs. Tynan.

MILDRED: God knows for what, Mr. Humphries, but you're welcome. (*As she goes*) God knows for what.

DARKNESS

ACT ONE

SCENE TWO

Now we are in the living room of Lulu Ames's suite in the Hotel Marlowe. It is half an hour later.

The suite is one of the best in the hotel. One door leads to the corridor and the elevators. Another door leads to the bedroom and bath. The walls are of a pale green and adorned with pictures of ladies of the French court in swings propelled by their beaux. There is a fireplace with a marble mantelpiece on which there is an ormolu clock. There is a small desk with a telephone and writing materials, a sofa, the usual chairs and tables, and a coffee table. The high windows with their generous moldings look out over the city; at night we can see the lights in distant apartment buildings. The furniture and fabrics, as in all hotels, don't quite match. The room is staid and impersonal, but somehow agreeable. There must be ten thousand such rooms in the older and quieter hotels in New York.

When the light comes up we discover several of Lulu's bags and a hatbox in the corner; her black coat has been thrown over a chair. There is a pot of yellow chrysanthemums on the coffee table, another on the mantelpiece. A tray of glasses and a bottle of champagne in an ice-bucket are on a table. Robert Ames is at the corridor door and is just letting in his wife, Betsy. Robert is twenty-seven, handsome, and already has begun to get a little heavy. Betsy is about twenty-six, good-looking and earnest—perhaps a tri-fle too earnest. She is dressed simply and extremely well in a tailored suit and sable scarf.

ROBERT: Hello, Betts.

BETSY: Hello, Bob. How are you, darling?

They kiss.

ROBERT (*closing the door*): Mother will be right out. She's just taking off her hat.

BETSY: How is she?

ROBERT: Wonderful. Crest of the wave.

BETSY (*taking off her gloves*): Why didn't she let us know the train, so we could meet her?

ROBERT: She didn't want to bother us.

BETSY: People wouldn't bother you if they didn't make such a point of *not* bothering you!

ROBERT: Ah, come on, Betsy. Mother's got no cinch now. She's all alone. Let's stop criticizing her and give her a good time. It's just for a little while.

LULU'S VOICE: (*offstage; calling through the closed door*): Bob, are you talking to somebody?

ROBERT: Just your only daughter-in-law!

LULU'S VOICE: Betsy, I'll be right in! How are you? And how's the baby?

BETSY: Hello, Mother Ames! I'm fine, and Christopher is not a baby! He is a man of three!

LULU'S VOICE: I take it back! I beg his pardon!

BETSY (*to Robert*): That's something she really must not do. It's bad for him to be called a baby. It makes him feel inferior.

ROBERT: He could stand a little of that. Darling, did you call the Calhouns?

BETSY: Bobby, I just couldn't bring myself to do it. Their dinner is so important to you. After all, there will be other nights for your mother. She'll understand. How long is she going to be here?

ROBERT: I don't know. She was so excited about arriving, I couldn't ask how soon she was going to leave.

BETSY: No, of course not. (*She goes to the telephone.*) Wait a minute. I want to call and see how the baby is. Good Lord, did you hear what I just called him? (*Into the telephone*) Plaza five, five-one-four-eight. (*She notices the champagne.*) What's all this?

ROBERT: Mother's idea; she ordered it before she got her coat off. No family reunion without champagne.

BETSY: Ah, why couldn't she have come yesterday or to-morrow? We could have had a real party for her. (*Into the telephone*) Hello, Lydia. This is Mrs. Ames. How's Christopher? . . . Has he had his supper? . . . Did he reject his carrots? . . . Well, that doesn't matter, just so long as you didn't force him. Did he finish his finger painting? . . . Well, you tell him his daddy and I will be home in a little while to see it. . . . All right, Lydia. Give him my love.

She is replacing the telephone as Lulu enters from the bed-room, carrying the dog.

LULU: Betsy, I'm so glad to see you!
BETSY: Mother Ames!

She starts toward Lulu, then gives a little shriek, quickly backs behind a chair.

LULU: What's the matter?
BETSY: It's the dog! I don't dare to come near the dog!
LULU (*bewildered*): But she's the friendliest little thing that ever lived.
BETSY: It's not that. If I as much as touched a dog I couldn't go home. Christopher is so allergic to dogs that his little face would swell up like a red balloon. (*Frowning*) Bob, you didn't touch it, did you?

ROBERT: Why, of course I did, Betsy. It was love at first sight.

BETSY: Oh, Bob! Well, you'll just have to take off your clothes in the living room before you go in to see Christopher. And that suit will have to go right to the cleaners. I'm sorry, Mother Ames, but if you knew what it was like!

LULU: I'm sorry too. I'll put her back in the bedroom. (*To the dog*) Come on, sweetheart; you take a little nap. (*She goes into the bedroom with the dog.*)

ROBERT (*calling after Lulu*): Tell her I'll bring her in a glass of champagne. (*The telephone rings.*) I'll get it, Mother. (*Into the telephone*) Hello. . . . Yes. . . . Oh, how do you do, Mrs. Mercer? Yes, Mother's here. Please come in. (*He hangs up. Lulu comes back into the room.*) That was Connie Mercer. She's coming in.

LULU (*to Betsy*): Connie and I were at school together a hundred years ago. She lives in this hotel. I wired her, and she got me these rooms. Aren't they nice?

ROBERT: She's a good-looking woman. At least she was. I haven't seen her since the last time you were in New York.

LULU: I'm sure she hasn't changed. Connie wouldn't.

ROBERT: You don't change much yourself, glamour puss. Now, Betsy, *you* say something nice to my mother.

BETSY: Mother Ames, you look absolutely wonderful.

LULU: You couldn't say anything I'd rather hear.

BETSY: But you look different, somehow. Oh, I know. It's the black. I've never seen you in black before.

ROBERT: My wife is noted for her tact.

LULU: I loathe the idea of mourning, but it seems to be expected of you. No, Betsy, I don't think you ever did see me in black. Bob's father disliked it so. Oh, at first I used to wear it now and then, just so he'd take some notice of me—if only to ask me to change my dress.

ROBERT: Mother, you make Father sound like a monster.

LULU: Do I, dear?

ROBERT: Father was a busy man. He had a great many things on his mind.

LULU: Only one. From the very beginning he was unfaithful to me.

BETSY (*shocked*): Mother Ames!

LULU: Oh, yes, he was in love with his business. He even slept with it three or four times a week—you remember that bed he had in his inner office.

ROBERT: Well, he was wrapped up in his business, I can't deny that. But it seems rather exaggerated, now he's dead, to go around accusing him of unfaithfulness.

LULU: Oh, I don't do that. This is just in the family.

ROBERT: After all, you did accept it. You did go on living under the same roof with him, didn't you?

LULU: You must remember, my son, you come of extremely conventional people. There's never been a divorce in the history of the family. Just the same, I had made up my mind to leave your father. (*With a little laugh*) Oh, no, Betsy, there wasn't anybody else. There just wasn't any Elliott.

ROBERT: And what happened to that plan?

LULU: Your father's illness, dear.

BETSY: You were so sweet with him, Mother Ames.

LULU: It wasn't hard. Illness was becoming to Elliott. It seemed to relax him. Bob, Bob, don't look so gloomy. It isn't all a horror story. There were nice things, you know. When you were a baby, and then when you were a little boy before you went away to school. After that, there were other things. Oh, hope, for instance; and then a sort of inertia, I suppose. And then, every day, of course, all the puttering little errands that make you think you're doing something. The days were slow, but the years went quickly. This last six months—since Elliott died—I've begun to realize how quickly. There are not too many left. Still, there are quite a few, aren't there? Now let's get off this. Somebody ask me, did I have a nice trip? I had a glorious trip. I was on my way to New York (*There is a knock on the corridor door; Lulu goes to answer it*) and my little dog wasn't trainsick for a moment, and— (*She opens the door*) Connie!

Connie Mercer enters. She is Lulu's age, and indeed a good-looking woman who is smart rather than handsome. Her clothes are simple but notable, and she is extremely well groomed. She carries a pot of chrysanthemums.

CONNIE: Lulu, I'm so glad! (*She notices the other chrysanthemums.*) Well, I got here just in time with these, didn't I?

LULU: I love them! (*She indicates the other pots of chrysanthemums.*) Those are from my children, those are from the management, and these are from you. Three pots of chrysanthemums all at once. Do you suppose New York's going to be like this every day?

ROBERT: Hello, Mrs. Mercer. It's good to see you again. Here, I'll take the flowers.

LULU: Put them here, Bob. (*She indicates the table.*) Connie, this is Bob's wife, Betsy.

CONNIE: Oh, yes, Christopher's mother. Well, whichever one he looks like, he can't go wrong.

Robert goes to the bucket, starts to open the champagne.

LULU: Connie, how are you? How's the job? (*To Betsy*) She doesn't look it, but she's a working girl. Interior decorating, if that's work.

CONNIE: That's work. The job's fine if you like lampshades. And I do, thank heavens. Except that one. Who designs hotel lampshades anyway? What drunken barber? Lulu, let me take a look at you. You look great. (*She shakes her head.*) No, no, my dear child. A show of grief is a seemly thing, but no woman has to go so far as to wear black stockings.

LULU (*anxiously*): Is it Akron, Connie?

CONNIE: Yes, sweetheart, it's Akron.

BETSY: Did you come from Akron too, Mrs. Mercer?

CONNIE: Oh, a long time ago. When I lived there nobody was safe from buffaloes.

ROBERT: How's your husband, Mrs. Mercer?

LULU (*distressed*): Bob! Ben died three years ago!

ROBERT (*to Connie*): Oh, forgive me. I didn't know. I'm so sorry!

CONNIE: You don't have to be sorry, Bob. Nobody's got to be sorry about Ben Mercer. He had a good life, he enjoyed every minute of it, and he died like *that*. (*She snaps her fingers.*) Tell me what more anybody can ask.

LULU: Connie, you're wonderful.

CONNIE: No, I'm not, Lulu. Ben was, and we had a fine time together.

Robert pours champagne.

ROBERT: A superb butler was lost when I became a lawyer. (*He hands Connie a glass of champagne, then gives Lulu one.*) Mother.

LULU: Thank you.

BETSY: Promise you're going to make it a nice long visit this time, Mother Ames.

LULU: I promise rather more than that, Betsy. I plan to stay here forever.

ROBERT (*pouring champagne into glass Betsy is holding*): Hold your glass steady, baby. (*After he finishes pouring, to Lulu*) Now, pretty lady, would you mind saying that over slowly?

LULU: I'm going to live here. I'm going to live in New York. I've burned all my bridges, and the smoke smells lovely.

CONNIE: Why, Lulu!

LULU: I didn't write you, Bob, because you might have written back. I didn't want any advice. I did it. And I did it forever. (*She rises in a sudden burst of elation.*) Oh, I'm going to love it here!

ROBERT: What did you do with the house?

LULU: I turned everything over to Tom Linscott. The house is up for sale—the furniture too, if anybody will buy it. (*A trifle defiantly*) I know; you think it's crazy; but I don't. Oh, everybody out there was perfectly dear, of course. There wasn't a day when two or three of them didn't call me up. "Lulu, don't sit alone in that dark house on this beautiful afternoon. Let me drive you out to the cemetery." And once one dear soul got me out there and said, "There's just enough room for you beside him. I hate a big plot."

BETSY: Mother Ames, it seems so sudden. Are you quite sure you've thought it out? Are you quite sure you shouldn't have waited awhile?

CONNIE: Waited for what?

LULU: Exactly! For what? Look, Bob, I'm strong and well. There are years to come for me, and I don't want them going past me empty. I'm still young, Bob, I'm still young.

ROBERT: You bet you are, and I'm glad you've done it. (*He goes over, kisses her.*) Nice work, glamour puss.

There is a knock on the corridor door.

LULU: Yes? Who is it?

BETSY: I'll go.

LULU (*as Betsy crosses to the door*): Maybe it's more chrysanthemums.

BETSY (*opening the door*): It's the maid, Mother Ames.

Irma enters. She is in her thirties, strong and healthy and good-humored. She wears a fresh linen uniform, and carries towels over her arm.

IRMA: Is it all right to turn down the beds now?

LULU: Yes, please. Come right in.

IRMA: Shall I turn them both down?

LULU: No, just one, thank you. (*As Irma crosses to the bed-room*) And there's a little dog in there, very friendly. (*After Irma is out, Lulu turns with delight to Robert and Betsy.*) Now isn't that glorious? The years I had to remind Phoebe to do it every night, and she does it without even being asked!

BETSY: Mother Ames, what do you think you'll do in New York?

LULU: I've got friends here, Betsy. Connie counts ten. And I hope to see something of you two and Christopher. After all, you're my roots. But I don't want to be a pest to you. And I don't want you to be a pest to me.

BETSY: You won't want to live in a hotel, will you?

LULU: That's just what I do want, Betsy. No more house-keeping, no more counting linens, no more following servants around, no more looking for dust. (*She runs her finger over the mantelpiece.*) Oh—

CONNIE: That's our New York dust. Specialty of the town.

LULU: It's sacred soil to me. Oh, yes, and another thing I'm not going to do. Never another stitch of needlepoint. I made a seat for every chair in that house. Wreaths of roses and lilies for people to plant their behinds on.

CONNIE: Oh, those women who do needlepoint! The shops are full of them—choosing their patterns and buying their wools. Well, I suppose it's one substitute for sex.

BETSY: Do you—do you think you might marry again?

ROBERT: That's the girl, Betsy. If you want to know something, you just go ahead and ask.

LULU: I don't know, Betsy. The subject hasn't come up. (*Irma comes out of the bedroom, starts toward the door leading to the corridor.*) Oh, just a minute. Bob! (*She pantomimes to Robert to tip Irma.*)

ROBERT (*handing Irma a tip*): Here you are.

IRMA: Thank you. (*To Lulu*) That's a darling little dog you've got in there.

LULU: Yes, isn't she nice?

Irma goes.

CONNIE: Lulu, you don't have to tip every time. Not if you're staying here.

LULU: I don't know a thing about tipping. Tipping and buying tickets and things like that—men's things. Bob, give Betsy some champagne. The poor girl's sitting there neglected.

BETSY (*to Robert*): No, darling, we really must go. We've got to go home and dress.

LULU: Oh, let's don't dress. Let's just stay as we are. You'll have to tell me a nice place to have dinner, but remember it's my party—my first night here. Connie, will you come along?

CONNIE: No, child, I have a date. I made it on purpose. Your first night here—that's for your family.

ROBERT ⎤ (*at the same time*): ⎡Why, you see, Mother—
BETSY ⎦   ⎣You see, Mother Ames, we—

ROBERT: Sorry, Betsy.

BETSY: It's all right, Bob. You go ahead.

ROBERT: You see, Mother, you gave us such short notice— We had this dinner engagement—it's going to be good and dull, too—but it was made a week ago, and we just couldn't get out of it.

LULU: Oh.

BETSY: It isn't just that it would be awkward getting out of it, Mother Ames, but it's so important for Bob. It's at the Willis Calhouns'. Their house. And Bob's been dying to get him for a client. It would mean so much.

LULU: Business first, of course.

ROBERT: You're sure you understand, Mother?

LULU: There'll be lots of other nights. Now go ahead. You mustn't think of being late. (*She goes to the door with them.*)

BETSY: I'll call you in the morning, Mother Ames. And we'll settle when you're to see Christopher. And, oh, Mother Ames, when you come to see him—

LULU: Yes, I know. I'll leave my little dog here. And Betsy, for heaven's sweet sake, will you stop calling me Mother Ames? It makes me sound like the top brass in a convent. Good night, kids.

ROBERT: Good night, Mother. Good night, Mrs. Mercer.

CONNIE: Good night.

They are out. Lulu closes the door, turns to Connie.

LULU: Connie, are you allergic to dogs?

CONNIE: No.

LULU: God bless you! (*She goes to the bedroom door and opens it.*) Come on in, honey. (*She picks up the dog.*) Yes, yes, yes, yes, yes. Well, I'm glad to see you too.

Connie crosses to where Lulu and the dog are having their reunion.

CONNIE (*patting the dog*): What's her name? Queenie?

LULU: I should say not. Her name is Sassy.

CONNIE: I knew it would be one or the other. Any girl dog west of the Hudson is either Queenie or Sassy. How long have you had her?

LULU: I got her right after Elliott died. And from the moment she came to live with me I've been putty in her paws. (*To Sassy*) What's the matter, honey? (*To Connie*) It's way after her dinnertime. She must be starved. (*She takes a can of dog food and a can-opener from a suitcase and looks at them helplessly.*)

CONNIE (*taking can and can-opener*): I'll do that. What do you know about machinery?

Connie starts to open the can while Lulu takes a plate from the suitcase.

LULU: And here's Sassy's plate. She simply won't eat off anything else. I've tried regular dog dishes—I've even tried Elliott's best Coalport china—but no. If she can't have her food on her five-and-ten-cent-store plate she won't eat.

CONNIE (*handing Lulu the open can*): Now you see how wrong first impressions can be. I thought she was a snob.

LULU: Oh, thanks. Come on, Sassy, dinner's being served.

With the plate and the can of dog food Lulu goes into the bedroom, carrying the dog. Left alone for a moment, Connie lights a cigarette. Lulu returns from the bedroom.

LULU: There. Now all's well. Poor darling, I don't know what I'm going to do if I ever have to go out without her. When she's left alone she howls.

CONNIE: Who doesn't?

LULU: But she does it out loud. Connie, who do you see? What do you do evenings?

CONNIE: Collapse mostly. I really do work like a horse. My boss is an idiot, and the rest of the staff is four young men who go to pieces easily. Even when they're in the best of health you have to stand on their insteps to keep them from flying away.

LULU: It sounds simply awful. But it doesn't seem to hurt you. You look wonderful.

CONNIE: Well, there's something delightfully soothing about the rhythm of that weekly check. Ben didn't leave a nickel, poor dear.

LULU: Maybe that was a good thing for you.

CONNIE: Shut your face, Lulu. That's what rich people always say. As a matter of fact, it was a good thing for me. I really love the job; I just complain to show off. Even aside from the money, I don't know what I'd do without it. It may not be the rich full life, but it's turned out to be a darn good one for me.

LULU: Is there a man, Connie?

CONNIE: No; oh, no. After Ben died there was a long stretch when I sat and looked at the wall. Then, a long

time after that, there was a man—a lovely man. I was
young again.

LULU (*gently*): What happened, Connie?

CONNIE: He found somebody who was young for the first
time. So then there was a succession of transients. If that
shocks you, Lulu, it shouldn't. The one-night stands don't
do any good; I found that out. There's got to be fondness,
and there's got to be hope. Lulu, please—this new life must
be all you want it to be. Only don't let yourself get lonely.
Loneliness makes ladies our age do the goddamnedest
things.

LULU: See that I don't, Connie.

CONNIE: I will. I'll watch over you. What am I talking about
anyway? You're good-looking and have pots of money.
Why should anybody worry about you? Honey, I've got
to go.

LULU: You're an angel to have got these rooms. I love them.

CONNIE: Well, any complaints, remember I'm right down the
corridor.

LULU: Good. We can have pillow fights and fudge makes.

They go to the corridor door.

CONNIE: I hate leaving you alone like this. Are you sure
you'll be all right?

LULU: Yes. It's just come over me that I'm awfully tired. After
all, this was a big day for me, perhaps the biggest I've ever
had.

CONNIE: I'll call you tomorrow. And kiss Sassy good night
for me. I'm glad you're both here. (*She kisses Lulu.*)

LULU: Good night, Connie. (*Connie goes. Lulu turns back
into the room, suddenly realizes she's all alone; she moves
about restlessly, then goes to the bedroom door, opens it,
chirps for Sassy.*) Here, Sassy. (*The dog comes in. Lulu
picks her up. Then, with the dog in her arm, she goes to the
light switch, snaps it off. Now the room is in darkness save*

for the light from the street below and the neighboring buildings. Lulu goes to the window with Sassy.) Look, Sassy. Look at all the lights. We're in New York, little dog; we're here. It doesn't matter what anybody says. It doesn't matter what anybody does. We did it, Sassy, we did it.

DARKNESS

ACT ONE

SCENE THREE

The corridor of the tenth floor in the Hotel Marlowe. It is morning, about ten o'clock, a week or so later.

There are three doors in a row, and the corridor trails off into shadows beyond them. Newspapers and mail are in front of each door.

As the light comes up, Mrs. Lauterbach opens her door, bends down, and picks up her newspaper and mail. She is wearing a wrapper and slippers. She is opening a letter when Mrs. Gordon appears at the door of her room. She wears a wrapper, and her hair is set with combs and covered with a coarse net.

MRS. GORDON (*cheerfully*): Hi, there. What's new on the Rialto? Well, I see you got a letter.

MRS. LAUTERBACH (*reading the letter, dispirited*): From my daughter. Afraid I'm not going up there for Thanksgiving. She says they feel they ought to go to his people.

MRS. GORDON: Well, that's good. You can keep me company. Of course, I've had any number of invitations to go away, but I say no, thank you. I just hate to leave my own bathroom.

MRS. LAUTERBACH: Maybe Christmas. It isn't so far away. (*Trying to pull herself together*) Well, fair lady. Sleepest thou well or sleepest thou ill?

MRS. GORDON: I went right through.

Mrs. Gordon steps away from her door, looks down the corridor.

MRS. LAUTERBACH: I didn't do so good myself. It was on my mind about that little blue ashtray. I just hate to have anything missing from my room. It gives me a nasty feeling.

Irma appears, carrying a dust-mop and carpet sweeper.

MRS. GORDON: Good morning, Irma. I see Mrs. Tynan has that "do not disturb" sign on her door again. Anything the matter?

IRMA: No, she just wants to rest.

MRS. GORDON: Is that what she told you to say?

IRMA: That's what she said, Mrs. Gordon. (*Irma goes on.*)

MRS. GORDON: Irma's getting spoiled.

MRS. LAUTERBACH: There's never any good behind those "do not disturb" signs. I remember when I first came here there was a lady living right on this corridor. Viola Hasbrook. She was a big Shakespeare actress—one of the biggest—but she retired—

MRS. GORDON (*glancing at her paper*): Yes, Mrs. Lauterbach, you told me.

MRS. LAUTERBACH (*going right on*): She just shut herself in her suite and she never went out. Years she stayed in there, can you imagine?

MRS. GORDON (*still looking at the paper*): My.

MRS. LAUTERBACH: And then once the "do not disturb" sign was up so long they got worried, and they went in, and there she was, sitting up dead. I saw them carrying her out in a basket. I was standing on this very spot. The maid who went in to clean up—oh, this was long before Irma—told me she had all the mirrors covered up like she didn't want to see herself.

MRS. GORDON: Certainly a lot of queer people in this world.

MRS. LAUTERBACH: And you know what? She must have had some kind of feeling or something. The switchboard operator we had then told me that she used to phone down—oh, in the middle of the night sometimes—that in case she died she wanted three embalmers, one after another. She was so scared she might be buried alive.

MRS. GORDON: Don't do for a lady to keep by herself like that. Makes her kind of nutty. (*Connie appears in street dress; she is on her way to work.*) Out bright and early as usual.

CONNIE: That's right.

She goes. There is a brief silence as the two ladies wait, making sure she is out of earshot.

MRS. GORDON: Off to business again. Funny thing, I never seemed to care much for ladies who work. Makes them kind of hard.

MRS. LAUTERBACH: I guess she has to. Her husband didn't leave her anything.

MRS. GORDON: Well, she has only herself to blame. Married woman ought to make her husband look ahead. Nobody lasts forever.

Mrs. Lauterbach steps away from her door and looks down the corridor.

MRS. LAUTERBACH: I see Mrs. Ames has taken in her paper already. She's up early every day.

MRS. GORDON: She'll get over that.

MRS. LAUTERBACH: When are you going in to pay your call of welcome on her?

MRS. GORDON: Soon as I have time. (*The third door opens, and Charles Nichols appears; he wears a dressing gown and slippers.*) Good morning, Charlie.

CHARLES: Good morning, ladies. (*He picks up his newspaper and mail.*)

MRS. LAUTERBACH: How's your sweet mother this morning?

CHARLES: Fine, thanks.

MRS. GORDON: Did she sleep good?

CHARLES: Very comfortably, thank you. (*He goes back into his room.*)

MRS. LAUTERBACH: I wish I'd had a comfortable night. That blue ashtray just seems to nag at me. Not that it was worth much, but it was so cute and pretty. Why, you know, Mrs. Gordon, you were admiring it yesterday when you were in my place.

MRS. GORDON: Oh, it'll turn up.

MRS. LAUTERBACH: I don't know. I lifted everything and shook it.

MRS. GORDON: Well, what's on for today?

MRS. LAUTERBACH: I thought I'd drop in at the bank. I haven't been there all week. I want to talk to my nice Mr. Kelly. What are you going to do?

MRS. GORDON: I've got to take that new girdle back. It didn't do anything for me. Maybe we could meet afterwards and have a sandwich at Schrafft's and go to a movie.

MRS. LAUTERBACH: Oh, that's a good idea. I hate a day with nothing to do. (*Turning toward her door*) Now I must go in and water my poor ivy. Poor little sing dets so sirsty. Plants really are a terrible care. Still, they're kind of company. Well, anything that needs you—

She enters her room, closes the door. Mrs. Gordon is about to enter her room when Lulu appears in street dress; she is still in black, except for her stockings and gloves, which are beige.

MRS. GORDON: Oh, Mrs. Ames, now I got you. You must think I'm terrible, not being neighborly with you, but I just thought I'd give you a week or so to get settled. Of course, we've spoken in the elevator, and I've patted your precious little dog. Where is he?

LULU: Out for a walk with that nice bellboy. And my dog is a little girl.

MRS. GORDON: I always call dogs he. It don't do to notice everything. (*Cackles.*) Now I know your name. I'll bet you don't know mine. I'm Mrs. Gordon. Virginia Gordon. My real name's Maude, but I tell everybody to call me Virginia. It suits me.

LULU: Yes, it does, doesn't it?

MRS. GORDON: Now how'd you guess I was Southern? Like it here at the Marlowe, honey?

LULU: Oh, very much.

MRS. GORDON: Did you have that other twin bed taken out of your bedroom?

LULU: Why, no.

MRS. GORDON: You should have done that first thing, honey. Nothing so depressing as an empty bed alongside of you all night. You mustn't let yourself get lonesome, you know.

LULU: Yes, I've been warned about that.

MRS. GORDON: Any time you do, you just come right to us. We've got a nice little clique all our own. (*"Clique" is pronounced "click."*) there's Mrs. Lauterbach, she lives in there. (*She indicates Mrs. Lauterbach's door.*) She's a Jew, of course, but she's real sweet. We just think she's one of us. (*Indicates another door.*) And Mrs. Nichols and her son are in that one. They have one of the two-bedroom apartments. There's plenty of means there. Maybe you noticed her; she's kind of noticeable. She's confined to a wheelchair; arthritic condition. But she's a real good sport about it; full of fun.

LULU: Who is that pretty little woman I see in the elevator sometimes?

MRS. GORDON: Mrs. Ames, you wouldn't want to know her. She isn't one of us. You'd think she'd be better off in some boarding house. Well, you know the old saying—too poor to paint, too proud to whitewash. Think you'd like to come to a movie this afternoon?

LULU: I'm afraid I'm busy.

MRS. GORDON: Well, how about this evening? We go to the movies almost every evening.

LULU: I'm afraid I can't tonight either.

MRS. GORDON: That's right, honey. Keep going as long as you can. But remember, here we are, waiting for you. (*She gives Lulu a girlish smile, starts to go back into her room.*)

DARKNESS

ACT ONE

SCENE FOUR

Now we are in the living room of the Nichols' suite. It is an afternoon some days later.

The living room has the same proportions as Lulu's, but we don't see as much of it. It is also much differently furnished. Mrs. Nichols is rich, and the furniture, which is her own, reflects her means. It is all heavy and covered with tapestry. On a table to one side are several large stamp albums, a magnifying glass, transparent envelopes of stamps and stickers.

When the light comes up we discover Mrs. Nichols, in a velvet teagown, seated in her wheelchair and reading the evening newspaper. Charles Nichols has just entered and is taking off his overcoat.

MRS. NICHOLS: Have a nice time, Charles?

CHARLES: Yes, thanks.

MRS. NICHOLS: The animals as charming as ever?

CHARLES: They're all right.

MRS. NICHOLS: Was it cold?

CHARLES: It was colder than it was.

MRS. NICHOLS: You didn't get a chill, did you?

CHARLES: No. (*He disappears into his bedroom.*)

MRS. NICHOLS (*calling after him*): If you were to get cold and couldn't go out, I don't know what those animals would do. Why don't you have a little sherry, Charles?

CHARLES'S VOICE (*offstage*): No, thanks.

MRS. NICHOLS: Oh, go on, have a little. Best to be on the safe side.

CHARLES'S VOICE: Grace, I told you I didn't want any.

MRS. NICHOLS: Well, there isn't much news to tell. The lobby was very quiet this afternoon.

CHARLES'S VOICE: That so?

MRS. NICHOLS: That Mrs. Tynan, she went through. Got out of her room for a change. I wish she'd get a new coat. That thing she has on can't even be warm.

CHARLES'S VOICE: No, it's colder than it was.

MRS. NICHOLS: Oh, Charles, stop woolgathering and come in here. (*Charles enters.*) Go on, change your mind about the sherry.

CHARLES: Grace, I told you I didn't want any. Will you kindly believe me?

MRS. NICHOLS (*handing him the paper*): Do you want the paper?

CHARLES: If you're through with it. (*He sits in a chair behind her.*)

MRS. NICHOLS: You know that stock Mr. Hubbard was pestering me to buy? Well, it's down another point and a half today. A good thing I didn't listen to him. Charles, do you think I ought to change brokers? Of course, I've had him all these years, but still— Well, I never pay attention to him anyway. Do you know people who have a green thumb with flowers? I have one with investments, thank heavens. Nobody could say that about your poor father.

CHARLES (*reading the paper*): You never have.

MRS. NICHOLS: He used to say we had enough money. He couldn't understand that he ought to make money into more money. I was the one who had to take over and do that. Well, he was a dear man. Sweet—not strong, but awfully sweet.

CHARLES: The way you like your tea.

MRS. NICHOLS: Charles, you idiot. Oh, well, I might as well keep Hubbard on and let him take my orders. Don't you think so, Charles?

CHARLES (*reading*): Hm-mm.

MRS. NICHOLS (*pleasantly*): Oh, stop your grunting at me and come around here where I can see you. (*Charles obeys.*) There, that's better. Find anything interesting in the paper?

CHARLES: Nothing much.

MRS. NICHOLS: That's the way it struck me. Dull. I think it's a little chilly in here. Don't you want to get my shawl?

CHARLES (*rising, going for the shawl, which is a scarf of rare lace*): I'll get it, Grace. Only please stop asking me, "don't I want to?" Just ask me, "will I?"

MRS. NICHOLS (*as Charles puts the scarf around her shoulders*): Just put it around my shoulder, will you? See, I didn't say, "don't you want to?" this time. (*Charles picks up his paper, sits down again.*) You seem a little downcast this evening. Anything happen?

CHARLES: No. What could happen?

MRS. NICHOLS: Would it cheer you up to go to the movies tonight?

CHARLES: Whatever you want.

MRS. NICHOLS: Well, we'll see how we feel later on. Dear me, it seems to me the ladies go to the movies every night. Well, maybe I would too if I didn't have you to talk to me, you old chatterbox, you. Well, shall we get to our stamps now? We've got a while before dinner.

CHARLES (*putting down the paper again*): If you like.

He rises, pushes his mother's chair to the table with the albums on it. He places a chair opposite her and sits down.

MRS. NICHOLS: The ladies can't get over me collecting stamps. I told them I made myself get into it because you were interested—and now I'm as bad as you are. (*Charles opens the albums as Mrs. Nichols picks up a transparent envelope and begins to take out the stamps.*) New Zealand, King Edward VII, one penny, carmine. (*Charles turns to a page.*) Here you are, dear.

She hands him the stamp. But instead of taking it, Charles suddenly pushes away the album and looks directly at her.

CHARLES: No— Grace, I want to tell you something, and I don't know any way to do it except just tell you. I want to get out of this.

MRS. NICHOLS: Oh, dear. I'm afraid it will be hard to find another hotel as nice as the Marlowe.

CHARLES: I'm talking about the whole thing. I've got to get out of it.

MRS. NICHOLS (*after a moment*): Yes, I knew there was something troubling you, but I didn't realize— Charlie, have I done anything to offend you?

CHARLES: Of course not, Grace.

MRS. NICHOLS: Aren't you comfortable here?

CHARLES: Of course I'm comfortable. I have a good bed, excellent food, and a dry roof. Oh, yes, and an expensive hobby. (*He indicates the stamp albums.*) But that isn't what I want. At least, I don't want it any more. I've had enough. I—

MRS. NICHOLS: Go on, Charlie. Surely we can talk.

CHARLES: Don't you see what it is? Here are two people in a small space, living one life. Your life isn't enough for me, Grace. I want my own.

MRS. NICHOLS: What will you do?

CHARLES: Teach.

MRS. NICHOLS: Oh, teach.

CHARLES: It's the one thing I know how to do. It's the one thing I like to do.

MRS. NICHOLS: It's eight years since you taught, isn't it? I imagine methods have changed in that time. But perhaps not in the teaching of English. If you should get a job, would you live here with me?

CHARLES: No, that's the whole thing.

MRS. NICHOLS: I see.

CHARLES: Of course I'd come to see you.

MRS. NICHOLS: I see.

CHARLES: And before I leave, of course, I'll arrange for the right nurse or companion. It's quite possible to get the right person when you can afford it.

MRS. NICHOLS: I can afford it, Charlie.

CHARLES: It would be so much better. Taking care of you— it's woman's work.

MRS. NICHOLS: Well, I can't say this surprises me. I've seen all the signs of this restless fit that's been coming on you.

CHARLES: It isn't just a fit.

MRS. NICHOLS: I'm sorry I used the wrong word. (*She picks up the magnifying glass, goes back to inspecting the stamps.*) My dear, they've cheated us. This is really a second-rate lot. Full of duplicates. Here's another from Liberia. Does teaching pay any better than it used to?

CHARLES (*lighting a cigarette*): Not much.

MRS. NICHOLS: Of course, when you taught before you lived at home. No rent, no food bills . . . Wait a moment! This looks like a Cape of Good Hope triangle. Hand me the catalogue. (*Charles hands her the catalogue.*) Thank you, dear. (*She looks through the catalogue.*) Well, the animals in the zoo will miss you. How did you say they were today?

CHARLES: Fine.

MRS. NICHOLS: All in their nice clean cages, nice and warm?

CHARLES: Yes, certainly.

MRS. NICHOLS: Poor caged things. And yet they say that when one of them escapes he's frightened out of his wits. He doesn't know what to do. Why is that, Charlie?

CHARLES: Give it up, Grace.

MRS. NICHOLS: Too much soft living, I expect. And too much care—yes, and affection. I've always heard the keepers are extremely fond of them.

CHARLES: Stop it, will you? You don't have to spell it out with alphabet blocks!

MRS. NICHOLS: Well, I can't find this stamp now. My eyes are tired. I think I'll go and lie down until dinner. Push me into my bedroom, will you? (*Charles puts out his cigarette, goes behind her chair.*) Let's have a particularly good dinner tonight, shall we? And perhaps a nice little bottle of wine.

CHARLES: If you want. (*He begins to push her toward the bedroom.*)

MRS. NICHOLS: Not to celebrate your new plans, but just because there's something so cosy about a really good dinner on a cold November night.

DARKNESS

ACT ONE

SCENE FIVE

Mildred Tynan's room. It is a week or so later, about noon.

The room is small and dark. There are a single bed, a bureau with a mirror over it, a chair, and a card table, and not much more. A single window looks out on a brick wall of a neighboring apartment building:

When the light comes up we discover Mildred lying on the unmade bed. She wears a skirt and blouse and bedroom slippers. A game of solitaire is laid out on the card table, and the blind at the window is down, even with the sill. Irma has just entered with carpet sweeper, pail, and dustcloths.

IRMA: Did you have your breakfast, Mrs. Tynan?

MILDRED: No, I just can't get to the drugstore. I got the just can'ts, Irma. I just can't get up; just can't get dressed; just can't go out. (*She indicates her blouse and skirt.*) I got this far, and then they got me again.

IRMA: Now you sit in this chair and let me make your bed. (*She pulls up the blind, then goes over to Mildred.*) Come on, Mrs. Tynan.

MILDRED (*rising from the bed*): Irma, you're a pest.

Irma begins to make the bed; Mildred goes to the bureau, opens a drawer, takes out a bottle.

IRMA: It's a lovely day out.

MILDRED: Is it? You tell me about it.

IRMA: Why don't you put on your shoes and coat and take a nice walk?

MILDRED (*holding up the bottle*): I thought there was a drink left in here, but no. (*She drops the bottle into the basket.*)

IRMA: Ah, that doesn't do any good.

MILDRED: Yes, it does, Irma. It makes you a different person. You're not yourself for a little while, and that's velvet.

IRMA: I tell you it doesn't help.

MILDRED: I tell you it does. A couple of drinks, and I've got some nerve. Otherwise I'm frightened all the time.

IRMA (*as to a child*): Now what is there for you to be scared of?

MILDRED: Everything. The dark. Morning. Tonight. Tomorrow. Next week. Forever.

Irma has finished making the bed.

IRMA: Want me to put these cards away, or do you want to finish your game?

MILDRED: Put them away, Irma. I'm giving up solitaire. I can't win even when I cheat.

IRMA (*gathering the cards together*): Get yourself cheered up, Mrs. Tynan. Go out and see some friends.

MILDRED: All my friends are in this room.

IRMA: Oh, I don't believe that for a minute. You must have lots of friends.

MILDRED: Oh, sure, once I used to have lots of them. At least, I mean I knew a lot of people. I had eight bridesmaids at my wedding. Pale green chiffon and yellow roses. They say green is unlucky, but I didn't know that until after. Beautiful, they looked. And all the time they were walking up the aisle of that church they were hating me because they all wanted to marry John Tynan. They couldn't understand why he had picked me—and neither could I. But I didn't look so bad myself that day.

IRMA: I'll bet you were a lovely bride.

MILDRED: I was, Irma, honestly I was. I was all white and innocent, and I was sort of shining because I was so happy.

IRMA: Ah.

MILDRED: Oh, Lord, I was in love with him. Being married to him, I couldn't believe it. I couldn't believe things could ever be rotten. And when I found out— (*She gestures helplessly.*) Well, I kept hoping, hoping. I'm the damnedest hoper you ever saw in your life, Irma. I can hope about anything.

IRMA: Why don't you get yourself something to do? It's bad for you to stay in this room all alone by yourself.

MILDRED: What could I do, for instance?

IRMA: There's all kinds of jobs. It would give you an interest.

MILDRED: Look, Irma, when I got away from California I thought sure I was going to get a job. And I did, too. I lasted three days. I was a saleswoman in a department store, except I couldn't keep my salesbook straight. That was the extent of my working career. After that I kept going and asking for jobs, but they never even said for me to come back. I guess I was so scared I scared them.

IRMA: Well, just because it was that way before doesn't say it would be now. Bad luck doesn't last forever.

MILDRED: Say it again, Irma. It's got to change.

IRMA: There must be lots of jobs around not too hard. The newspapers are full of them.

MILDRED: Do you really think so? Do you honestly?

IRMA: Well, I can tell you about my niece, right in my own family. There she was, young and just out of high school, didn't know a thing. And the first ad she answered, she got a job. The very first.

MILDRED: Do you think that could happen to me? You do, don't you? Well, so do I! I told you I was a hoper, Irma. It's all right to hope if you've got something to hope about.

(*She goes to the telephone and speaks into it.*) Would you ask Harry if he would go out and get something for me?

IRMA: Ah, Mrs. Tynan.

MILDRED: Don't worry, Irma. I feel too good now to need a drink. (*Then into the telephone*) Will you ask Harry to get me a morning paper? . . . Thank you. (*She hangs up.*) Irma, you've made me feel lucky. I'm going to follow it right up. (*She gets her shoes, puts them on.*) You see, when I get a job it's not going to be just for something to do. I need that money, you know I do. And maybe I'll be able to save some. And if I saved some, then I could get a divorce. It's horrible, hanging on like this. He said he would never give me one, but maybe if he saw I was making my own money, and he saw he couldn't keep me on a leash any more—well, he'd see it was no use. I'll bet he would! I'll bet he would! . . . Wouldn't he?

IRMA: It's an awful nice feeling, making your own money.

MILDRED: Oh, it will be, won't it? Irma, don't fuss with the room any more. Go on, tell my fortune for me. Tell me how lucky I'm going to be. (*She picks up the cards, shuffles them.*)

IRMA: Well— (*She puts down her dustcloth.*) I hope I'll see something nice.

MILDRED: I know you will; I just have a feeling. Here. (*She hands Irma the cards.*)

IRMA (*cutting the cards into four stacks, reciting as she lays each down*): To your house; to your heart; to your fortune; to your wish. You make your wish and hold on to it.

MILDRED (*eagerly*): You think I won't!

IRMA (*beginning to lay out the cards*): Oh, this looks pretty good. Look at all those diamonds! There's the ten, and there's the queen, and one right after the other. That's money right around you.

MILDRED: Honestly, Irma?

IRMA: The cards don't lie, Mrs. Tynan. And there's your wish card, right near you.

MILDRED: Oh, that's wonderful! I've got that job right now!

IRMA: Sh! Don't tell me what you wished, Mrs. Tynan. That's not good.

MILDRED (*dismayed*): Did I spoil it?

IRMA: Just don't tell anyone. Now shuffle these once. (*Mildred does.*) Now wish hard. (*Irma cuts the cards.*) Oh, you're going to get it, Mrs. Tynan.

MILDRED: God bless you, Irma. Don't tell me any more. I just wanted to know about that wish. (*As Irma gathers the cards*) Irma, would you do me a favor? Would you sew a button on my coat? (*She goes to her coat, which is over a chair.*)

IRMA: All right, Mrs. Tynan. As soon as I finish the corridor.

MILDRED: No, do it now. If I see that job in the paper I'll have to go right out.

IRMA: Where's the button?

MILDRED: In the pocket. It's been there for days. Oh, won't it be wonderful when I can buy some new clothes? And Mr. Humphries, poor little man, he'll fall over in a faint when I pay him the whole bill all at once. (*Irma begins to sew on the button.*) Irma, you're an angel. I suppose I really ought to get a manicure. Well, I can't, I'm too broke. I'll have to keep my gloves on. Isn't it lucky I washed my hair last night? Wish I had a new lipstick. I never liked this color. (*She looks into the mirror.*) Lord, the first time I've really looked at myself in the mirror for ages. It isn't so good, but it'll have to do.

IRMA: Oh, you look nice, Mrs. Tynan.

MILDRED: Well, it isn't going to be my looks anyway; it's my talents. Let's see. What are my talents? What do I think I'm going to do anyway? Think I could teach French? I used to speak very nice French, all in the present tense. Maybe I could give music lessons to backward children. There must be lots of backward children around. I took music lessons for years. I finally got so I could play the "Minute Waltz" in a minute and a half. No, no fooling, what can I do? Oh, I do know. I can arrange flowers.

I'm really a whiz at that. People would come to our house and see my arrangements and say I must have Japanese blood in me. That was before the war, of course. Irma, haven't you always heard that people get paid a lot of money for arranging flowers? I'm sure I've seen something in a magazine about it. Haven't you? I'll bet there'll be an ad today. Somebody wants a flower arranger immediately.

IRMA (*finishing with the button*): Here you are.

MILDRED: Thank you, Irma. Wait a minute. (*She takes her handbag from the bureau, offers Irma a dollar bill.*) Here.

IRMA: No, you wait until things get better.

MILDRED: They're going to right away. I've got a hunch. (*Irma shakes her head. There is a knock at the door.*) That must be Harry now. (*She opens the door. Harry enters with a folded newspaper.*) Hello, Harry.

HARRY: Good morning, Mrs. Tynan. Here's your paper.

MILDRED: Thanks ever so much. And here. (*She gives Harry the bill.*)

HARRY (*reaching into his pocket*): I think I've got change.

MILDRED: Oh, no. No change. All yours.

HARRY: Thank you. (*He goes.*)

IRMA: Honestly, Mrs. Tynan, giving Harry a dollar for a newspaper!

MILDRED: Oh, but this is the newspaper that's going to change everything. And Harry's such a nice boy. Everybody's a nice boy today. (*She is looking through the newspaper.*) Where are the want ads anyway? Don't they want people to read them? How do they expect you to get a job? Take it all back. Here they are. (*With a deep breath*) Here we go, Irma. Keep your fingers crossed.

There is a silence. The silence lengthens.

IRMA: See anything that sounds good?

MILDRED: Listen— (*Then, reading in a dull voice*) "College graduates—teletypers—electronics—study to be an airplane hostess—photographer's model—five feet, eight, thirty-six, twenty-four, thirty-six—accountants, experienced—stenographers, experienced—tearoom hostesses, experienced—beauticians, experienced—young women—young women—girls—girls—girls . . ."

DARKNESS

ACT ONE

SCENE SIX

The living room of Lulu Ames's suite. It is several days later, about six o'clock in the evening.

The room is pretty much the same as when we saw it the first time, save that now there are books and magazines. Glasses, an ice-bucket, and bottles of liquor are on a table; Sassy's plate is on the mantelpiece. Perhaps the most conspicuous additions are a needlepoint frame and a great bag of colored wools.

When the light comes up we discover Lulu and Robert. Lulu wears a simple afternoon dress of some pale soft color. Robert, who is seated on the sofa and has a drink in his hand, seems worried and depressed.

LULU: Bob, this is nothing so terrible. So Betsy and I had a quarrel last night at your house. These things happen in families all the time.

ROBERT: I know, but I can't help feeling sorry. I just wanted to tell you that.

LULU: Want another piece of ice, dear?

ROBERT: No, thanks, this is fine. Look, Mother, about last night. I admit Betsy can be difficult, but there are times when you are no cinch yourself.

LULU: Really, dear? What do I do?

ROBERT: It's not what you do. It's what you won't do. You

won't interpret Betsy. I admit she hasn't got the gift for saying things prettily, but she's worried about you.

LULU: What on earth is she worried about me for?

ROBERT: Perhaps partly because I am. Mother, you've got to
occupy yourself. You've got to find something to do.

LULU: So Betsy told me last night. So she told me between
thirty and forty times, as I remember. But I don't recall either you or she suggesting just what I should do.

ROBERT: You didn't give us the chance, really.

LULU: All right; you've got the chance now.

ROBERT: Well, that's rather hard to say—

LULU: Isn't it? (*Patting his hand affectionately*) Bob, you're
feeling guilty because you're not holding my hand every
second. Honestly, I don't want that.

ROBERT: Well, it feels like worry to me, because as I see it
there isn't much difference between your life here and your
life in Akron.

LULU: Oh, yes, there is. The difference is that I'm not in
Akron. The difference is that something could happen here.
Look, Bob, would you honestly feel any better if I was taking a course in art appreciation at Columbia? Or did you
have in mind something nobler? Such as volunteering to
run the switchboard in a hospital?

ROBERT: My God, how you would louse up a switchboard.

LULU: Bob, there really isn't a thing I can do. And because I
know I can't, I've come to believe I don't want to. And by
now, my son, I believe that very firmly.

ROBERT (*doggedly*): But you just can't let yourself go to
waste. It's criminal.

LULU (*smiling*): All right, then leave me to my life of crime,
and you stop worrying. And Betsy too. And next time I see
her, I promise I'll interpret her.

ROBERT: Mother, come home with me. Come have dinner
with us tonight.

LULU: Darling, I can't. Connie Mercer and I are going to the
theater.

ROBERT: You two are going alone?

LULU: We'll protect each other. Now how about you? How are daytime things? How is the majesty of the law?

ROBERT: There wasn't much law today. I've been talking to agents about a possible house in the country. Connecticut or Westchester. It would be so good for the children.

LULU: Children?

ROBERT: We're going to have another baby.

LULU (*surprised and delighted*): Oh, Bob, that's wonderful! Here we've been sitting talking about idiotic little squabbles, and all the time you knew this.

ROBERT: We haven't told anybody. If you announce it too soon, at the end of a couple of months people go around saying, "Hasn't she had that damn baby yet?"

LULU: Tell Betsy how delighted I am, will you, Bob? And I'll call her up and tell her myself.

ROBERT: I wish you'd do that, Mother. Thank you. You don't feel hurt about our moving away from the city?

LULU: Why on earth should I? We live in a wonderful age. (*There is a knock; Lulu crosses to the corridor door.*) I believe they even have things called trains. Oh, come in, Con.

Connie enters. She is in street clothes and wears a hat.

ROBERT: Hello, Mrs. Mercer.

CONNIE: Hello, Bob.

LULU: How are you, Connie? Have a drink? What would you like?

CONNIE: Cyanide on the rocks.

LULU: What's the matter?

CONNIE: I'm stuck, Lulu. I can't go to the theater tonight. The boss broke it to me just as I was leaving. A lot of new stuff has come in, and we've got to get it marked and on display. Damn these weeks before Christmas, anyway. (*Robert has gone over to the table where the liquor is.*) Oh, Bob, I can't take time to have a drink, but I'm going to. Scotch and soda would be wonderful.

LULU: I'm so sorry about tonight.

CONNIE: So am I. The place is hell on wheels lately. One of the daffodils had a breakdown and had to go to a sanatorium. He could have got out a week ago, but he wanted to finish weaving his mats.

LULU: What are you going to do about dinner?

CONNIE: I'll get a sandwich at the drugstore. I came home to put on low heels; there'll be no sitting down tonight. Oh, thanks, Bob. (*She takes a drink from Robert.*)

ROBERT: Mother, if Mrs. Mercer has to work, why don't you come and have dinner with us?

LULU: No, dear, later in the week. Let the smoke of the battle die down.

ROBERT: I wish you'd come. Well— (*He picks up his hat and coat, which are over a chair.*) Good-by, Mrs. Mercer. Mother, we'll see you soon.

LULU (*going to the door with him*): Please do, dear. Oh, and Bob. Get a lovely house. One you'll love. And if you think it costs too much, here I am.

ROBERT: Thanks, Mother. (*He kisses her, then goes.*)

CONNIE (*pointing to the needlepoint as Lulu comes back into the room*): Lulu Ames, what does this mean?

LULU: I know. I was the one who said I'd never do another stitch, but I couldn't resist the design. It's so pretty.

CONNIE: Uh-huh, lilies and roses. Have you gone back to your old ways?

LULU: No, just tapering off.

CONNIE (*pushing off her shoes*): Ah, there, that's better. How are you, Mrs. A.? I haven't seen you since you were a little girl.

LULU: Don't I know. It's awful never seeing you.

During the next several speeches, Lulu takes Sassy's plate and a can of dog food from the mantelpiece and begins to fix Sassy's dinner.

CONNIE: Bob looks fine.

LULU: He is fine. I'm very fond of him.

CONNIE: How's what he's married to?

LULU: He likes her.

CONNIE: Who else have you been seeing besides your loved ones? Anybody we used to know? What about May Talbot? Is she any thinner?

LULU: I imagine considerably. She's been dead for two years.

CONNIE: Oh, heavens. Who else? Who's alive?

LULU: Most of those who are, aren't in New York. The Blakes have gone to live in Nassau. And Laura Stevens—she lives in California. The Martins have settled in London.

CONNIE: I know. That's what happens. You expect people to stay put, but they either die or go on shorter journeys. Is there anybody left?

LULU: Only in a way. I've seen a few of them, but they're all so old. It's too depressing. (*There is a knock on the corridor door; Lulu goes to answer it.*) Excuse me. That must be Sassy.

CONNIE: You know her knock?

LULU: Of course I do. (*She opens the door. Harry enters with Sassy on a leash. Lulu picks up the dog.*) Did she walk nicely, Harry?

HARRY: For the grandstands, Mrs. Ames. Thousands cheered.

LULU: Thank you. (*As Harry starts to go*) Oh, Harry, we can't use those theater tickets tonight. Do you think they'd take them back?

HARRY: Well, I'll call the broker, but it's pretty late.

LULU: Don't worry about it. It isn't so terrible if they don't. (*He goes. Lulu closes the door. To the dog*) Did you have a nice time, baby? Connie, do you think she looks a little pale?

CONNIE: Oh, Lulu, her cheeks are blooming.

LULU: I don't know. She hasn't been herself. Maybe it's all the people and the noise. I wish she'd get used to New York. (*To Sassy*) Sassy, will you eat your dinner? Will you do me that one little favor and eat your dinner and then take a nice nap? (*She takes the plate which she has fixed, goes into the bedroom.*) Right back, Connie. (*The telephone rings.*) Answer it, will you, dear?

CONNIE (*into the telephone*): Hello . . . Oh, would you wait just a moment? (*Calling to Lulu*) Lulu, there's a Mr. Osgood downstairs. Do you want him to come up?

LULU'S VOICE (*from the other room, through the open door*): Oh, I forgot all about him! Yes, please, Con!

CONNIE (*into the telephone*): Will you ask him to come up? (*She hangs up as Lulu comes back into the room.*) Well, what have we here, Lulu?

LULU: Little Paul Osgood—Claire Osgood's baby brother. He called me yesterday, so I asked him in for a drink. I suppose Claire wrote him that I was here. You remember Claire, don't you? (*She takes Connie's glass.*)

CONNIE: Is she still going? She must be a hundred and ten.

LULU: No, she isn't; she just looks it and acts it.

CONNIE: What's the kid brother doing in New York?

LULU: Oh, he's been here a long time. He has a bookshop. He was married to an awfully pretty girl—Sally something-or-other. They're divorced now. I don't know what happened, but, Lord, how Claire Osgood hates her. (*She hands Connie a fresh drink.*)

CONNIE: Thanks, Lulu. What else have you been doing? Have you met any of our ladies in the hotel?

LULU: They've met me more than halfway. They keep urging me to go to the movies with them.

CONNIE: Don't you do it. Those women are dead, and death is contagious.

LULU: They're just poor things.

CONNIE: Poor things—that's the least they are. Lulu, have you been lonely at all?

Lulu is about to reply, seems to have difficulty finding the words. She is released by a knock on the corridor door. She goes to answer it.

LULU (*as she crosses*): How can I be lonely when I have my Sassy? (*Opening the door*) Good heavens, look what I called little Paul Osgood.

Paul Osgood enters. He is thirty-eight, tall, and wears his excellent clothes casually.

PAUL: How do you do, Mrs. Ames?

LULU: Come in, Paul. It's all right to call you Paul, isn't it?

PAUL: Please do.

LULU (*to Connie*): Look at it. The last time I saw it, it was at the cap-pistol age and with one of the dirtiest faces ever exhibited in Ohio.

PAUL: You had a great influence on me, Mrs. Ames. It was because of you that I took up soap and water. I had a terrible crush on you, but you—you never knew. (*To Connie*) How do you do? My name is Paul Osgood.

LULU: Oh, I'm sorry. This is Mrs. Mercer, another refugee from Akron.

CONNIE: (*indicating her stocking feet*): Pardon this little eccentricity of mine. I always take my shoes off when I drink.

PAUL: I think it's a very pretty custom. (*He puts his overcoat over a chair.*)

LULU: Let me make you a drink, Paul. And aren't you going to ask me about your sister? How she is?

PAUL: I think I know, unless she's broken something within the last few hours. (*To Connie*) My sister is what is called accident-prone, Mrs. Mercer. Her wrists and ankles are constantly snapping like an open fire.

CONNIE: Oh, poor dear.

PAUL: Yes, perhaps. I hadn't thought of it that way. But perhaps.

LULU (*handing Paul a drink*): Paul, you didn't know my son Bob in Akron, did you?

PAUL: No, but I learn about him from Claire's letters. Lulu Ames's son is the successful lawyer, and I'm the bum in the bookshop.

LULU: I may as well break it to you. Claire still refers to you as her baby brother.

PAUL: You're not the first to tell me, Mrs. Ames. What's it called when you murder your sister?

CONNIE: Where is your bookshop, Mr. Osgood?

PAUL: Just two blocks from here. An ideal location. A branch of the public library is right around the corner.

LULU: Is it attractive?

PAUL: I hope you'll come see it and tell me.

CONNIE (*rising*): Well, I've got to get back to the salt mines. (*She picks up her bag and shoes.*) Good-by, Mr. Osgood. I'll come in and buy some books as soon as I learn to read.

PAUL: Thank God that doesn't stop most of my customers. Good-by, Mrs. Mercer.

CONNIE: Good-by, Lulu. So sorry about tonight.

LULU: Stop thinking about it. (*They kiss.*) Call me when you have a moment. (*Connie goes.*)

PAUL: Mrs. Ames, you may think this verges on the personal, but I never saw anyone like you. You haven't changed a bit.

LULU: Oh, that's very dull of me. People ought to change.

PAUL: Not if they're lovely to begin with.

LULU: I'm afraid you are verging on the personal. I like it. You've certainly changed since I've seen you.

PAUL: Of course I have. I've lived a couple of thousand years.

LULU (*hesitantly*): I—I was sorry to hear about you and Sally.

PAUL: I was too.

LULU (*giving him a quick look, then changing the subject*): Claire's told me so much about the bookshop. What a pleasant job that must be. And it's doing well, isn't it?

PAUL: Very well indeed. I'm thinking of selling it.

LULU: But that doesn't go together. It's doing very well, and you're thinking of selling it. Now why?

PAUL: For the same reason I gave up the apartment and went to live at the University Club. For the same reason that I keep away from all the people Sally and I used to know. I don't want any reminders.

LULU: What will you do if you sell the bookshop?

PAUL: I believe I'll go to Mexico. You see, Sally was never in Mexico.

LULU: But what would you do there?

PAUL: What other expatriates do. Become a beachcomber without a beach.

LULU: Oh, Paul, you mustn't do that.

PAUL: Did you ever see Sally, Mrs. Ames?

LULU: No. I saw her picture in the paper at the time you were married. She was simply beautiful.

PAUL: Simply beautiful. She was, she is. The beauty that makes you imagine there is a heaven. And the mean heart, the tiny mind, the arrogant, vicious, greedy body that makes you know there is a hell. And if she wanted me to tomorrow, I'd take her back like a shot. So, as you see, I'm in great shape.

LULU (*troubled*): Paul, my dear, it's bad for you to be so bitter.

PAUL: I know. Hatred's filling, but it isn't nourishing. At the moment, my former wife is doing splendidly. She married a captain in the Army and is living in Japan. They have a charming place and six houseboys. She is about to engage a seventh.

LULU: Seven houseboys? What on earth for?

PAUL: There are seven nights in the week, Mrs. Ames.

LULU (*shocked*): Oh!

PAUL: I never thought I'd be sorry for a captain in the Army. Poor son of a bitch.

LULU (*looking down at her drink*): I hope you haven't noticed them, but there are still wisps of wheat in my hair. Out where I've come from, we don't speak quite so freely.

PAUL: Sorry, Mrs. Ames.

LULU: Paul, it can't all be bad memories. You must have had something in common.

PAUL: Sure we did. We were both in love with her. Of course I didn't realize this until after the divorce. The divorce went off admirably. One of those perfectly friendly things, you know. Each just wished the other was dead.

LULU: Oh, dear.

PAUL: I've talked rather excessively about myself. It's your own fault, you know. You have the kind of face that makes people confide in you. Well, let's draw you into the conversation. How do you like New York? How long are you going to stay? What have you been doing? Have you seen all the new plays? Have you done the art galleries? Are you comfortable here at this hotel? And what's the number on my watch?

LULU: Yes.

PAUL: That clears up everything about you.

LULU: Well, I have left out something. I'm just a little bit disappointed in New York.

PAUL: It isn't quite all you expected?

LULU: I suppose that's it. Though I don't know what I did expect.

PAUL: Probably what everybody expects when they first come here—excitement, interest, a feeling of being part of what's going on.

LULU: Well, it's my own fault. I asked so much.

PAUL: Don't stop that, Mrs. Ames. People who ask little usually settle for it.

LULU: Yes, I've seen that in the women in this hotel. They've settled for such a little bit.

PAUL: God, don't I know.

LULU (*surprised*): You do?

PAUL: There are lots of hotels around here, and the female inmates come into my shop—the lending-library part. Mrs. Ames, this is against my best business interest, but promise me you'll never be seen carrying a lending-library book— the book with the cellophane dust jacket. It's the badge of the unwanted woman.

LULU: I promise you, Paul.

PAUL (*rising*): And I promise you I'll say no more about my connubial experiences. God, aren't all words connected with marriage horrible? Connubial, nuptial, spouse. . . . And I'll promise you something else. Next time we'll talk entirely about you—if you'll permit a next time.

LULU: I hope there will be many, at least.

PAUL: Thank you. (*He goes toward his overcoat.*) And don't be disappointed in our city. It's doing the best it can.

LULU (*seeing the tickets on the desk*): Oh, Paul. I have two tickets for the theater tonight. Connie Mercer and I were going, but she has to work. Please, could you possibly use them? Or have you a date?

PAUL: No, I haven't.

LULU: Maybe there's someone you'd like to take.

PAUL: There certainly is. You.

LULU: Oh, now don't feel you have to—

PAUL: I never felt anything less. Mrs. Ames, would you do me the honor of accompanying me to the theater? And will you do me the immediate honor of being my guest at dinner?

LULU (*starts to protest*): Why— (*Then, with a smile*) Mrs. Elliott Ames accepts with pleasure Mr. Paul Osgood's kind invitation.

DARKNESS

CURTAIN

ACT TWO

ACT TWO

SCENE ONE

The lobby again. It is several months later. According to the clock back of the desk it is almost midnight. The lights are low; a faint glow comes from the direction of the street.

When the light comes up we discover Harry reading a newspaper which he has spread open on the counter. A portable radio is beside him, and while he reads he whistles along with softly playing dance music. Presently Charles comes from the direction of the elevators; he wears a raincoat and hat.

HARRY (*turning the radio down*): Hello, Mr. Nichols. Out to get the morning papers?

CHARLES: Think I can make it before the rain starts, Harry?

HARRY: Is it going to rain?

CHARLES: Unless it's going to snow. It feels like something.

Charles goes. Harry calls to an unseen room in back of the desk.

HARRY: Hey, Casey, better get the runner down! Charlie boy has one of his feelings!

He turns up the radio again, goes back to reading. Now Mrs. Gordon and Mrs. Lauterbach enter from the direction of the street.

MRS. GORDON: Good evening, Harry.

HARRY (*turning down the radio*): Good evening, ladies.

MRS. GORDON: Goodness, look at the time, will you? I thought the picture was long, but not that long.

MRS. LAUTERBACH: I won't be good for anything tomorrow. (*Harry gives the ladies their keys.*) Thank you, Harry.

HARRY: The picture good?

MRS. GORDON: One of those English things. They're all the same.

MRS. LAUTERBACH: Everybody running around on those moors again. Well, let us hie us hence, fair lady. Good night, Harry.

MRS. GORDON (*whose attention has been arrested by something at the front door*): Wait a second. I want to see this.

The ladies sit on the sofa. Lulu and Paul enter; they are in evening clothes.

LULU (*to the ladies*): Good evening.

MRS. GORDON ⎱ (*together*): Good evening.
MRS. LAUTERBACH ⎰

LULU (*going to the desk*): Does there happen to be a small poodle back here, Harry?

HARRY: Just a minute, Mrs. Ames. (*He disappears.*)

MRS. GORDON (*in a whisper to Mrs. Lauterbach*): Be talking, can't you?

MRS. LAUTERBACH (*a trifle too loud*): I don't think the coffee at that theater is as good as the coffee at the Esquire. Do you, Mrs. Gordon?

Harry reappears with Sassy.

LULU: There she is. (*She picks up Sassy; Paul pats the dog's head.*) Was she a good girl, Harry? Did she cry?

HARRY. Not a peep out of her, Mrs. Ames. And I had her out.

LULU: Thank you.

Lulu and Paul go in the direction of the elevators.

PAUL (*as they pass the ladies, patting Sassy*): Aren't you going to say hello to your uncle?

MRS. GORDON (*when they are out*): Now watch this! What do you bet he goes up?

MRS. LAUTERBACH: Oh, I don't think so.

MRS. GORDON: Well, you've got a sweeter mind than I have. After what I told you I heard last night at two a.m. this morning. Heard them talking in her room. Heard his voice just as plain.

MRS. LAUTERBACH: If they were talking it couldn't be anything bad.

MRS. GORDON: Oh, no? They can talk afterwards, can't they?

MRS. LAUTERBACH: I didn't think she was that kind.

MRS. GORDON: Well, still waters run dirty, you know. No, here he comes. He didn't go up. (*Louder, as Paul enters, goes toward the front door*) No, like you said, Mrs. Lauterbach, the coffee was pretty weak. But after all, when you get things free it don't do to complain. . . . Well, it's a good thing I didn't bet any money. Surprised it's lasted this long. (*Rises.*) Good night, Harry.

HARRY: Good night, ladies. (*They go in the direction of the elevators as Casey appears with the runner. He puts it down, begins to unroll it. Harry turns up the radio again, goes back to reading. Now Charles returns with several newspapers under his arm.*) Rain started, huh? You called the turn, all right.

CHARLES: I guess I did.

HARRY: I hope your mother has a good night.

CHARLES: Thank you. (*He goes in the direction of the elevators.*)

HARRY: Well, I guess I'll knock off.

CASEY (*glancing toward the front door*): Hey, listen to that rain!

HARRY (*folding the paper*): Yeah, I hate to go out in it. The one night in the week I pick to go home, and it's got to come down in buckets.

CASEY (*with a note of admiration*): A big week, huh?

HARRY: One of the biggest. The town's full of it. The way the dames are handing it to you, all you have to do is reach out and take it. Well, if they want to offer it to you on a platter with parsley around it, what are you going to do?

CASEY (*still looking toward the street*): Jesus! Look at that, will you? Damn fool! That car almost got her! Hey, it's Goldilocks.

HARRY: She's going to get hers one of these days. Why doesn't she look where she's going?

Mildred enters. She carries a quart bottle of liquor in a paper bag and wears fanciful high-heeled slippers without any stockings. Her hair is loosened and glistening with raindrops, and her cheeks are flushed. She is very drunk, but she seems happier and looks prettier than we have yet seen her. Her walk is uncertain, but as she hears the music from the radio she breaks into a little dance step. The tune is "Anchors Aweigh," and she sings the only words of it she knows.

MILDRED: "Anchors aweigh, Navy—anchors aweigh. Anchors a-a-a-a-wa-a-a-a-y!" (*She tries a rather more complicated dance, lurches, and saves herself by catching the desk. Harry snaps off the radio.*) Ah, Harry, just when I was having fun! (*She puts the bottle of liquor on the desk.*)

HARRY: It's such an old tune, Mrs. Tynan. They always give out with the dogs this time of night.

MILDRED: Sure it's old, but I got a sentimental feeling about it. Reminds me of the happiest time of my life—while he was away in the Navy. (*She opens her handbag.*) Oh, Harry, I got a little business to transact. I want to pay something on my bill.

HARRY: Why don't you let it go till morning when Mr. Humphries will be on?

MILDRED: No, no, this hotel has been very nice to me, and I want to do my share. (*She takes out an envelope.*) I've owed them a long time, and they haven't locked me out, and I appreciate it. Here, Harry, see if this is enough.

HARRY: Mrs. Tynan, wait until morning, then pay the cashier or Mr. Humphries. This isn't my job.

MILDRED: If I don't pay it right away, it will just go. You wait so long, then it goes so quick. Do you know when it came? This afternoon, air mail special delivery. Think they're doing me a favor—special delivery! (*She drops her handbag.*) Oh! Oh! Oh!

Casey bends down, picks up the bag.

CASEY: Here you are, Mrs. Tynan.

MILDRED: Thanks, Casey. (*She hands Casey a bill.*) Here.

CASEY: Oh, you don't have to do that, Mrs. Tynan.

MILDRED: Go on and take it. (*Back to Harry*) Are you going to let me pay my bill?

HARRY: I can't, Mrs. Tynan, it's not my job. Anyhow, I'm off duty now.

MILDRED: Oh, if it's on your spare time. I didn't know it was your spare time, Harry. I'm sorry. (*She turns on the radio.*) I'm on my spare time too. I've been celebrating my special delivery. Ask any bartender on Third Avenue: did I get my special delivery today? (*The music blares loudly.*)

HARRY (*going toward the radio*): Mrs. Tynan, you're going to get us in trouble! (*He snaps it off.*)

MILDRED: I wouldn't get you in trouble, Harry. Well, if there's not going to be any music, I guess I go upstairs. No music upstairs. Radio's busted. No anything upstairs.

She starts away from the desk, drops her bag again. As she leans to pick it up, she overbalances and falls flat. She makes no attempt to rise.

CASEY (*without moving*): Now what do we do?

Harry comes out from behind the desk, looks down at her.

HARRY: You all right, Mrs. Tynan?

MILDRED (*from the floor*): I'm fine. I like it here.

HARRY: Yeah, but you might catch cold. (*He picks her up under the arms expertly, puts her on her feet. As he does so her coat falls open, and we see she is wearing only a brassière and panties. She pulls the coat closed quickly.*) Can you walk all right?

MILDRED (*for a moment her dignity returns*): Yes, thank you. I slipped on the rug. I suppose my shoes were wet.

Casey shrugs, goes to the desk.

HARRY: Here's your bag. (*He takes the bottle from the desk where she has put it.*) And here's this.

MILDRED: Thank you, Harry. You're very kind.

HARRY: Want me to help you to the elevator?

MILDRED: Oh, no, thank you. It's not at all necessary.

HARRY: Good night.

MILDRED: Good night. (*She starts away, then turns back, pleading.*) Harry, come up and have a drink with me, won't you?

HARRY: I'd better not, Mrs. Tynan.

MILDRED: It's off duty. It's all right. (*Coaxing him*) You wouldn't want me to drink alone, would you?

HARRY: You must be tired, Mrs. Tynan.

MILDRED: I'm not tired. It's just I dread going up there for when the loneliness comes on. Please come, Harry. Please keep me from being lonely, just for a little while, will you, Harry?

HARRY (*after a moment*): Well, you go up. I'll come up in the service elevator in a couple of minutes.

MILDRED: Thank you, Harry. Thank you. (*She does not lurch now, but walks steadily to the elevator. Harry waits until she has gone, then looks over at the admiring Casey.*)

HARRY: Well, I don't go out in the rain, after all.

CASEY (*awed*): Jesus, right here in the hotel.

HARRY: On a platter with parsley, Casey, on a platter with parsley.

DARKNESS

ACT TWO

SCENE TWO

Lulu's living room again. It is some weeks later, about ten o'clock in the evening.

The hotel furniture has gone, and now the room reflects Lulu herself. The furnishings are English antiques of the more delicate periods, articles of which you see the beauty before their great cost strikes you. The colors of the upholstery and draperies are soft and glowing, and on the wall are two good oil paintings. Here and there are charmingly arranged bouquets. The room is elegant without being cold, feminine without being fussy. The needlepoint apparatus is no longer in evidence. Sassy's plate is no longer on the mantelpiece.

When the light comes up we discover Lulu and Paul Osgood, apparently hostess and host to Tom and Mary Linscott. Connie Mercer is the fifth member of the group. Mary Linscott is within a few years of Lulu's age, but looks a generation older. She has a pleasant face and a comfortably plump body. Tom Linscott is in his early sixties; he has taken good care of himself, and there is about him the self-assurance of success. He wears a dark business suit, and his wife has on a conservatively cut evening dress, obviously expensive, and even more obviously not smart. Connie wears a simple, very smart evening dress. Paul is in a dinner jacket. Lulu has come into a new radiance. She wears a brilliant evening gown, and there is a most becoming change in her coiffure. Her hair has been cut shorter and, without having at all the look of being bleached, is brighter.

LINSCOTT: It was the way I was saying to Mary. New York's all right, of course, but it's a lot easier to take when you can see old friends here. Only sorry I didn't bring my tux.

LULU: Paul, aren't you ashamed of yourself? Look at those empty glasses.

PAUL: All right, Lulu. Fire me the first of the month. (*Rising*) May I, Mrs. Linscott?

MARY: Oh, I couldn't. My, that dinner!

PAUL: How about you, Mr. Linscott?

LINSCOTT (*giving his glass to Paul*): Well—for the road then. Con, I never thought when I used to see you around with the other kids that you'd turn out to be a regular business-woman.

CONNIE: Neither did I.

LINSCOTT: Well, life certainly treats you fine.

CONNIE: No, Tom. Life and I go Dutch.

MARY: I wish we didn't have to go back tomorrow. Still, it will be nice to tell everybody about seeing you three. Paul, Claire will be delighted to hear how well you're looking. She's getting along splendidly. They're taking the cast off next week.

PAUL: She'll have another before she has time to miss it.

MARY: Oh, now, Paul.

PAUL (*giving Linscott his drink*): Here you are, Mr. Linscott. (*He turns to Lulu.*) Lulu?

LULU: Please.

Paul takes Lulu's glass, goes to refill it.

PAUL: You've been looking a little startled, Mrs. Linscott, every time I call her by her first name. I should have told you it was by request.

LULU: I had a terrible time making him do it. He says it's such an awful name.

PAUL: I didn't say that at all. I simply said it lacks a certain heroic quality.

MARY (*turning to Connie*): Can you get over the way Lulu looks? And her hair! Isn't it gorgeous?

LULU: It was Paul's idea.

PAUL: No, it wasn't. You asked me if you ought to have it done, and I said sure, go ahead.

LULU: It's the same thing.

MARY: And here, in a strange city, where nobody knows you well enough to criticize, it was very sensible to go out of mourning. Why should we mourn? Death isn't the end. Is it, Paul?

PAUL: I've been so busy, really I haven't had time to keep up with things. Has some new evidence come in?

Lulu giggles. Paul gives her a drink; as he does, she touches his hand affectionately. Both Mary Linscott and Connie notice this; Tom Linscott is lighting a cigarette and does not.

LINSCOTT: Well, Lulu, it looks like you're settled here.

MARY: That's what surprises me. I thought you'd try New York a little while, then you'd want to travel. You know, go around Europe.

LULU: Now how could I do that? I have a hard enough time buying tickets in English. What would I do, a woman alone in Europe? Sit in one hotel after another. Oh, I'd so much rather sit in a hotel here. (*With another affectionate glance at Paul*) New York turned out even better than I expected.

MARY: Well, you've got a lovely place here. But you know, I miss something. It doesn't seem like Lulu's room without her needlepoint bag and all her wools. My, Lulu did such beautiful work.

LULU: Yes, I did, didn't I? Oh, well, I suppose it's one of the substitutes for sex.

Connie looks at her. Lulu smiles sweetly in return.

LINSCOTT: Say, Lulu, I've been meaning to ask you. What's become of that cute little dog you had?

MARY: Yes, I thought you brought her with you. Why, Lulu, what's the matter, dear?

Lulu has begun to cry.

PAUL: Lulu, no!

LULU: Excuse me! (*She rises quickly, goes into the bedroom.*)

PAUL (*following her*): Lulu! Lulu, dear, please, don't! (*He enters the bedroom, closes the door. The Linscotts look at each other in bewildered silence.*)

MARY: What on earth—?

LINSCOTT: What did I do? I only asked her about the dog.

CONNIE: I should have managed to tell you before. Lulu's little dog died a few days ago. She's just heartbroken about it.

MARY: Oh, that's too bad. That really is. I remember how we felt when our old Queenie died.

LINSCOTT: It's like a member of the family.

MARY: Think I ought to go in? Or you, Connie?

CONNIE: I don't think so.

MARY: Well, I guess she's got the person she wants in there. What's this all about, Connie?

CONNIE: I don't think it's about anything at all. I think it's just nice for Lulu to have somebody take her out. It's a good thing for a woman to have a man to take her out.

LINSCOTT (*frowning*): Well, I don't know—

CONNIE: I do. It keeps you in practice. After a while you lose the knack if you don't. If you keep going out with other women you forget. When at last you do get out with a man, you find you're holding doors open for him, giving the waiter the order yourself, and all but picking up the tab.

MARY: I never saw such a change in anybody. That hair. Lulu Ames bleaching her hair. Poor Elliott must be spinning in his grave.

CONNIE: If he is, that's the first time he ever moved fast.

LINSCOTT: Come on, now, Connie.

MARY: Oh, I think her hair is wonderfully becoming. It's just that these things so often lead to foolishness. Let's see, Paul Osgood— (*Counting on her fingers*) He must be twelve years younger than Lulu, anyway.

CONNIE: Oh, nobody's younger than Lulu.

MARY: Well, I'm not surprised. When she decided to leave Akron I knew she was up to something.

CONNIE: Mary, Lulu's never up to anything. She can't make a plan. She's a creature of sudden impulses and long waits.

MARY: I guess she was in one of her long waits—if that's what you want to call it—all the time she was married to Elliott. She never did a thing. She would never join any of our lovely ladies' organizations. I used to beg her to, but no.

CONNIE: Mary, she just isn't that kind of person. Maybe it's her hard luck.

MARY: Well, I don't know what I'd do if I didn't keep busy. I tell you, Lulu's headed for trouble. Why couldn't she fall in love with somebody her own age?

CONNIE: Who said she was in love?

LINSCOTT: Well, I don't like it. Man works damn hard, leaves his wife all his money, and some pretty boy comes along and gets it. Sometimes I think those old East Indians had the right idea about widows. Cremate the husbands and burn up the wives along with them.

CONNIE: Maybe it would be simpler to burn up the money.

Paul enters from the bedroom.

PAUL: Lulu wants me to tell you she's so sorry.

CONNIE: I explained, Paul.

MARY: We understand.

PAUL: She knew you would. Mrs. Linscott, when you go back to Akron, will you tell my sister I don't hate her—I just hate writing letters?

MARY: Yes, we really must go, Tom. I'll tell her, Paul.

LINSCOTT: Connie, tell Lulu what a good time we had, will you? (*They start moving toward the door; Paul picks up Mary's wrap, helps her with it.*) That Persian Room certainly is quite a place. Coming, Osgood?

PAUL: I think I'll stay and see how Lulu is feeling.

CONNIE: I'll chaperon them, Tom.

MARY: Good-by, Connie, dear. Lovely to have seen you.

CONNIE (*as they kiss*): Good-by, my dear.

LINSCOTT: Good-by, Connie. Glad to hear you're doing so well. (*He looks coldly at Paul.*) Osgood.

They go. Connie closes the door.

PAUL: I thought they'd never go.

CONNIE: They do give that illusion. How's Lulu?

PAUL: She'll be all right in a minute. Do you think I eased them out too swiftly?

CONNIE: You got results.

PAUL: Won't you have a drink?

CONNIE: No, thanks.

PAUL (*fixing a drink for himself*): Good God, what an evening. Both of them looking daggers at me. Daggers, hell. Bayonets.

CONNIE: It's not you they resent, Paul. It's Lulu. She broke away from the tribe—and God knows that was bad enough. But she's happy—and that's unforgivable.

PAUL: Nice people.

CONNIE: Well, they really are, you know. And the thing is, they're genuinely fond of Lulu. Ah, here she is.

Lulu has entered from the bedroom.

LULU: I'm sorry, children. I'm such an amateur at crying, I don't know when to stop. Connie, where's your glass? Have a drink?

PAUL: I asked her, but she refused. (*To Connie*) She says she has to go.

CONNIE (*smiling*): Yes, I did, didn't I, Paul? (*She kisses Lulu.*) Good night, dear. God bless you.

LULU: He has. (*Connie goes. Immediately Lulu crosses to Paul, and they embrace.*) Darling— (*Then*) Wasn't it awful?

PAUL (*holding her in his arms*): It's getting better.

LULU: Poor Paul.

PAUL: Not now.

Paul kisses her again; they separate. Lulu goes to the sofa.

LULU: It was nice of Connie to come with us. It was even nicer of her to go and leave us alone.

PAUL: What have you been doing all day, Mrs. A.?

LULU: Hold on to your chair, it's pretty exciting. Well—this morning I had a manicure. Then I went mad and bought a big jar of bath salts. And then I came back and had lunch up here—consommé, mushroom omelet, and raspberry ice. After lunch I unwrapped my bath salts and saw they had given me rose geranium instead of verbena. So I had a cause. So I wrapped it up again and took it back to the shop and came home in triumph with my verbena. Still interested?

PAUL: Fascinated.

LULU: Then I took a long, long bath during which I debated with myself as to whether verbena was really so much more refreshing than rose geranium. Then I walked around the room, this room, sort of straightened the pictures, pinched the flowers, and the first thing I knew another hour had sped by like an iceberg. So then I got dressed and here I am. And now what did you do?

PAUL: Just the bookshop. I had lunch with Martha and Jack Pason. I hadn't seen them in months.

LULU (*after a slight pause, carefully*): Weren't they Sally's friends?

PAUL: Both Sally's and mine. Yes.

LULU: Was it difficult for you to see them again?

PAUL: Not in the least. Everything very easy and casual.

LULU: Did they say anything about her?

PAUL: I didn't ask for news.

LULU: Do you still think you might go to Mexico, Paul?

PAUL: Right now I wouldn't go to Mexico if they gave me the place and threw in Cortez. (*Coming over to her and taking her hand*) I'm well, Lulu. You did it. Thank you.

LULU: Do you know who I'd rather be than anybody in the world at this moment?

PAUL: Who?

LULU: Me. (*He kisses her.*) Do you think the Linscotts noticed anything?

PAUL: Only everything.

LULU: Now they'll tell everybody in Akron I'm a bad, bad woman, and none of them will ever come see me or speak to me again. (*A little cheer*) Yaaay! Oh, when I think of all those years in Akron—

PAUL: Don't look back. You'll turn to salt.

LULU: When I think of the narrow escape I had! Paul Osgood, do you realize I might have died without ever knowing what—it—it could be like—without ever knowing about this?

PAUL: I had my own narrow escape. That letter of Claire's telling me you were in New York. The first letter from her in years that I read all the way through.

LULU: Four months and three days now. Remember when I thought if I ever did what I did the skies would fall and the buses would stop running? And then that next morning when I looked out the window, the skies were never higher, and the buses were racing along one right after another.

PAUL: It simply shows you're not all that important.

LULU: I'm important to you, aren't I?

PAUL: If I can stand your grammar, I guess you must be. (*He rises.*)

LULU: Where are you going?

PAUL: Just to get a cigarette. (*He crosses to a table where there is a cigarette box.*) Look, Lulu, the Pasons want to know if you'd like to come to dinner next Thursday.

LULU: Oh, that's—that's very sweet of them.

PAUL: Will you come?

LULU: Oh, I don't think so, Paul. You go.

PAUL: But I want you to come with me. I want to show you off.

LULU: Ah, that's sweet. But just the same, I really don't think so.

PAUL: Why not?

LULU: I guess I'm scared to meet new people.

PAUL: Darling, didn't you come to New York to meet new people?

LULU: Yes, but then I met you, and so I don't want to meet anybody else.

PAUL: But that's no good, Lulu.

LULU: It isn't?

PAUL: Look, Lulu, two people, no matter what their feeling, mustn't feed entirely on each other. If they do, all that's left of them is a little heap of bones.

LULU: Even if they—if they're fond of each other?

PAUL: Especially if they are. What chamber of Dante's hell was it where Paolo and Francesca were floating on the wind, doomed to be locked in each other's arms for eternity?

LULU: I think it sounds lovely.

PAUL (*with a sigh*): Lulu, you're outrageous. Maybe that's why I like you.

LULU (*going up to him*): Tell me some other reasons. (*She puts her arms around him.*)

PAUL: What have I done? What have I done to be yoked to this?

LULU: Hey, you know what? I just thought. Paolo is the Italian for Paul, isn't it? Let's float on the wind.

He embraces her.

DARKNESS

ACT TWO

SCENE THREE

The living room of the Nichols' suite. It is several weeks later, about four o'clock in the afternoon.

When the light comes up we discover Mrs. Nichols seated in her wheelchair. An album is open in front of her, and she is inspecting a stamp with the aid of a magnifying glass. She is humming tunelessly, a picture of cheerful tranquillity. Presently there is a knock on the corridor door.

MRS. NICHOLS (*without looking up*): Charles, there's someone at the door, dear.

Charles enters from his bedroom. He is a much different Charles. He holds himself straighter, and his step is quicker. He goes to the door, admits Harry, who has a large box.

HARRY: A package, Mr. Nichols.

CHARLES: Wait a second, Harry.

MRS. NICHOLS (*still busy with the stamps*): Have you some change, dear? There's some on the desk. Good afternoon, Harry.

HARRY: Good afternoon, Mrs. Nichols. Are we going to see you down in the lobby later?

MRS. NICHOLS: I'm afraid not today, Harry. This isn't very good arthritis weather.

CHARLES (*taking a coin from the desk*): Here you are, Harry.

HARRY: Thanks, Mr. Nichols. (*He goes; Charles closes the door.*)

MRS. NICHOLS: That must be my new dressing gown, dear. Put it in my bedroom, will you?

CHARLES: No, it's something for me, Grace.

MRS. NICHOLS (*looking up*): Oh, really. What is it?

CHARLES: It's a new suit.

MRS. NICHOLS: Oh, how nice. Let me see it.

CHARLES: It's just a dark blue suit.

MRS. NICHOLS: Good. I like you in dark blue. Go on, let me see it. (*Charles opens the box, takes out the coat. Mrs. Nichols reaches out her hand, feels the material.*) Oh, that's very good. It's not just a dark blue suit at all. It's got that nice little pin stripe. I'm glad you got it, Charles. You were beginning to dress a little too quietly. After all, you're still a young man.

CHARLES: You don't think it's too young, do you?

MRS. NICHOLS: Put it on—the coat—and let's see how it fits. (*Charles takes off the coat he is wearing, puts on the new coat.*) When did you get it, dear?

CHARLES: One day last week when I was out. I didn't go to the zoo.

MRS. NICHOLS: You never said anything. Oh, I see, you wanted to surprise me. Charlie, I like it; I like it very much. Turn around. That left sleeve isn't too long, is it?

CHARLES: Is it?

MRS. NICHOLS: No, it's all right. I guess it was just the way you were holding your arm. I hope you won't try to wear it for a while, dear. It's more of a summer weight.

CHARLES (*taking off the coat*): I got it for the summer.

MRS. NICHOLS (*with a little laugh*): Why, Charles, that isn't like you, looking ahead. Well, hang up your nice new suit, dear, and then come help me with these. I'm rather afraid I'm bungling things—you've let me do it alone so much lately, and I'm no good without your help.

CHARLES (*picking up the box*): I will in just a few minutes, Grace. I want to finish a letter I'm writing.

MRS. NICHOLS: Goodness, you've been writing so many letters. Could they be about that job you wanted? You know—back before Christmas.

CHARLES: Yes, I have been applying for a job, Grace. And you've taken it wonderfully—never a word.

MRS. NICHOLS: My dear child, it's what you want to do. Charles, pour me a glass of sherry, will you?

CHARLES: Do you think you should?

MRS. NICHOLS: Oh, I don't have to tell the doctor everything. Have you had any answers to your applications?

CHARLES (*pouring sherry into two glasses*): Just notes, saying there were no vacancies on the faculty at present. But a pretty hopeful one came this morning. (*He brings the sherry over to where Mrs. Nichols is seated.*)

MRS. NICHOLS: Oh, good, you're having one with me. Thank you, dear. Well, tell me quick, what's the hopeful letter?

CHARLES: (*taking a letter out of his pocket*): It's from the Webster School in Connecticut. They need someone for their summer school to teach English to the younger boys.

MRS. NICHOLS: Ah, yes, the younger boys. I think I've heard of that school. It has a very good reputation, hasn't it?

CHARLES: It's got a fine rating.

MRS. NICHOLS: Yes, that's what I've heard. How on earth did you get in touch with them?

CHARLES: The way I did with the others. Just looked at the school advertisements in the magazines and wrote and asked if maybe they didn't want an English teacher.

MRS. NICHOLS: Oh, that was really enterprising, Charles. What did the Webster School say?

CHARLES (*handing her the letter*): The headmaster is to be in town next Wednesday, and I'm to let them know if it would be convenient for me to meet him at his hotel.

MRS. NICHOLS (*glancing at the letter*): Oh—Doctor

Nicholas Whittaker. Doctor of Divinity, I suppose. What a
nice letter. Well, I'm sure you're writing that it will be convenient, aren't you?

CHARLES: Oh, sure. It's none too early to make arrangements. Summer school starts the first of July and runs to
September.

MRS. NICHOLS: That's why the summer suit. (*She puts the
letter on the table.*) Yes, that's a lovely letter. It does sound
as if they're interested, doesn't it? Do the teachers get any
time off through the summer?

CHARLES: I imagine we get week ends now and then, so I'll
be able to come down and see you.

MRS. NICHOLS: Oh, I hope so.

CHARLES: Look, Grace, I wasn't going to tell you until I was
sure, but this letter makes me feel pretty certain. I went to
an agency, and I think I've found the ideal woman for you.
A sort of nurse-companion. As nice as she could be, and
she's had experience in cases like yours. I liked her the
minute I saw her.

MRS. NICHOLS: Oh, you've been away from the zoo quite a
bit, haven't you?

CHARLES: Well, I just couldn't think of walking out of here
without having you settled.

MRS. NICHOLS: Oh, I'm settled. You engaged her?

CHARLES: No, of course not, Grace. Not until you've seen
her. She's on a case now, but she'll telephone in the next
day or so. You'll want to talk to her, of course.

MRS. NICHOLS: I don't think so. I don't think it will be necessary.

CHARLES: Oh, Grace, you've got to find out if you like her.

MRS. NICHOLS: No.

CHARLES: Grace, come on. You can't take care of yourself.
Who'll push your chair? Who'll get you in and out of bed?
Who will give you your shots? Please be sensible.

MRS. NICHOLS: I will. I promise. (*She leans over, takes his
hand.*)

CHARLES: Well, I'd better finish my letter. I want to get it off this evening. (*He picks up the box again and starts for the bedroom.*)

MRS. NICHOLS (*going back to her stamps*): Oh, Charles.

CHARLES (*at the door*): Yes?

MRS. NICHOLS: When you wrote the Webster School, what did you say in your letter?

CHARLES: Why, I gave what I thought were my qualifications. I told them my school and college, and what experience I had had in teaching.

MRS. NICHOLS: You—didn't give them any references?

CHARLES: No, I didn't.

MRS. NICHOLS: Yes, of course you didn't. But when you go to see Doctor Whittaker—he'll undoubtedly ask for references, won't he?

CHARLES: Yes, he probably will.

MRS. NICHOLS: What will you do in that case?

CHARLES: I'll simply tell him I've been inactive for so long because I've been taking care of my mother.

MRS. NICHOLS: And I'm sure he'll admire you for your reason. Still, I think he will feel it necessary to write to the school where you taught and inquire about you. And what will happen then, do you think?

CHARLES: Nothing will happen. The school closed years ago, Grace.

MRS. NICHOLS: Schools close, but people's memories don't. The boy's parents are probably still alive—nasty people live forever. Remarkable we never heard any more from them. Every day I thought we might.

CHARLES: How would people ever hear?

MRS. NICHOLS: People hear, people hear. And it's always what you don't want them to hear.

CHARLES: That's that chance I'll have to take.

MRS. NICHOLS: Maybe we needn't worry about them. Maybe they'll go on keeping their promise. After all, I kept mine. I paid them that preposterous sum, and we left the town. Maybe that part is all right. But of course there are other matters.

CHARLES: What other matters?

MRS. NICHOLS: Why, Charles, what a curious thing to ask! The obligations of a human being.

CHARLES: Grace, what are you talking about?

MRS. NICHOLS: I'm talking about the most important thing of all—duty. Doctor Whittaker has a tremendous duty to those children. Those little boys are in his charge. He dare not expose them to—

CHARLES: To what?

MRS. NICHOLS: Need we go into that?

CHARLES: Are you telling me that you feel you have a duty?

MRS. NICHOLS: Yes, Charles, I am.

CHARLES: To whom?

MRS. NICHOLS: To those little children, Charles. As I get nearer the grave, I realize that I must do what is right, painful though it may be to me and mine. If you're not going to tell Doctor Whittaker the truth, then I must.

CHARLES: But it wasn't the truth! It was a vicious lie!

MRS. NICHOLS: Appearances, Charles, appearances.

CHARLES (flaring): And what were the appearances?

MRS. NICHOLS: You kept the boy after school.

CHARLES: I wanted to help him with his composition. All right, we were alone together in the schoolroom, but I never touched him.

MRS. NICHOLS: But it was appearances. They were so damaging. He was such a pretty little boy.

CHARLES: Grace why? Why this? I've paid my debt, surely, for the money you gave that boy's parents. For these years, do you know what I've been here, Grace? A Gray Lady. Duty—I know, duty. But can't it also be a duty to give someone a chance for a life?

MRS. NICHOLS: It's nice for you that you think it's all that one-sided, Charles. But suppose you listen to me for a minute. It wasn't too easy for me to give up my lovely home, all my friends, and come to a strange city. And where do you think this all came from? (She indicates herself in the wheelchair.) The doctor says that worry and fear could do it.

CHARLES: Grace, let me go! Let me go!

MRS. NICHOLS: My dear Charles, there's no question of letting. But if you do what I think is wrong, then I must do what I think is right.

CHARLES: Jesus Christ. Grace, for all this time you've kept this over me! You never spoke of it! You've been saving it for this!

MRS. NICHOLS: No, not exactly for this. But I realized that when you came to this age—a man, you know—restless, you know, restless. Yes, Charles, I was saving it. And if you ever get restless again, dear boy, I shall still have to do what I must do. (*She takes the letter from the table, hands it to him.*) You'll remember that, won't you?

Charles looks at the letter, sits down, slowly tears up the letter. Mrs. Nichols goes back to the album.

DARKNESS

ACT TWO

SCENE FOUR

The living room of Lulu Ames's suite. It is a month later, a little after seven o'clock in the evening.

The room is the same except for a different flower arrangement. Sassy's plate is again on the mantelpiece, and there is a large box on a chair. Two books in cellophane dust jackets are on the coffee table. A table is placed near the windows and set with a lace cloth, silver service for two, a low bowl of flowers, and crystal wineglasses. Tall white candles not yet lighted are in silver candlesticks, and two chairs are drawn up to the table. The effect is highly elegant yet extremely intimate.

When the light comes up we discover Lulu giving a last glance at the arrangements. She wears a charming teagown and looks her best. There is a knock on the corridor door.

LULU: Just a minute, darling! (*She goes to the record player, puts on a record. It is de Falla's "El Amor Brujo." Then she quickly goes to the table, lights the candles.*) I won't be a second. (*She gives the table a last quick look, touches a flower, then rushes to the door. Connie enters in street clothes and a hat.*)

CONNIE: Lulu, wait until I tell you!
LULU: Oh. Come in, Connie.

CONNIE: The most wonderful thing has happened! I'm a thousand miles up in the air. I'm jumping over little pink clouds.

LULU: Oh, really? What is it?

CONNIE: Well, that darling, dear, sweet, intelligent, humane boss of mine—

LULU: Just a minute, Con. (*She turns off the music, then goes and blows out the candles.*) Now tell me.

CONNIE: That blessed angel is sending me abroad. France and Italy and England. I'm going to buy furniture. I'm going to be gone for months with an expense account like a maharajah's.

LULU: Oh, that's lovely; perfectly lovely.

CONNIE: And do you know what else? When I come back I'm going to be a partner.

LULU: That's wonderful.

CONNIE: Sure it is, but I'll have to realize that later. I'm too excited about going to think about coming back. I honestly don't know what I'm doing. For heaven's sake give me a drink to sober me up. (*She goes to the table.*) Do you and Paul have dinner here every night?

LULU (*making a drink*): Not every night any more. He thinks it's wrong not to see something of other people.

CONNIE: Don't you see something of them too?

LULU: I tried. Honestly I did try. We went out three or four times with friends of his. But it all went wrong from the start. You see, these were people he knew when he was with Sally. I felt as if I was being compared.

CONNIE: Oh, Lulu, that imagination of yours!

LULU: That's what Paul said. He said it was silly. Well, maybe it was, but that's the way I felt. And there's something else I keep feeling: he's enough for me; why aren't I enough for him?

CONNIE: Did you say that to him?

LULU: Yes, I'm afraid I've said it to him a lot of times. He didn't like it. Connie, I didn't think it could happen, but

I've been making scenes. I always thought people who made scenes were disgusting. I still do. (*She goes to the window, looks down into the street.*)

CONNIE: Ah, Lulu, get hold of yourself.

LULU: Don't you think I've tried? (*She moves away from the window.*) Connie, I'm a pig; a filthy, self-centered pig. Here you are with your wonderful news, and I go spoiling your pleasure with my stupid tales of woe.

CONNIE: Please, Lulu. I'm all set. Now what we've got to do is get you fixed up.

LULU: I don't know how to get myself fixed up. There's something lacking. I guess there's something lacking in a lot of women; nobody's ever one of a kind. We were told you grew up, you got married, and there you were. And so we did, and so there we were. But our husbands, they were busy. We weren't part of their lives; and as we got older we weren't part of anybody's lives, and yet we never learned how to be alone. It's different with girls now. But that's the way it was with me. . . . Connie, do you really think it matters that a woman is older than a man?

CONNIE: Only if they think about it.

LULU: Paul doesn't think about it. I'm the one who does.

CONNIE: Then stop.

LULU: Nasty little thing. He's late again.

CONNIE: Lulu, you've got to get out of this.

LULU: I tried. (*She indicates the books on the coffee table.*) I took a big adventurous trip to the lending library. Oh, not Paul's. I didn't dare go to the one in his shop. He says the lending-library book is the badge of the unwanted woman. But I can't read, even mysteries. A beautiful young girl gets chopped into little pieces with an ax, and all I think is: And she thinks she's got trouble! No; more and more I just sit here and play my game.

CONNIE: What game?

LULU: I make believe Paul and I are going to be married. I

even decided what I would wear. I had a hard time choosing between beige and gray, but I think definitely gray. Not old-lady gray, you know. Sort of pinkish gray. And I think those little butterfly orchids. I love yellow and gray, don't you? Do you think I'm crazy?

CONNIE: Not quite.

LULU: Well, then, I'll show you I really am. Wait a second. (*She goes quickly into the bedroom. Connie looks after her, troubled. Lulu returns with a charming little gray hat with a veil floating from it.*) I saw exactly the right wedding hat, so I bought it.

CONNIE: Yes, it's darling. Lulu, why don't you come abroad with me?

LULU: No, Con. It's sweet of you, but I can't.

CONNIE: Sure you can. And don't think you'll be left alone. Look, I'll have time off. I'll take time off. Come on.

LULU: No, I've got to stay here. (*In a sudden outburst*) Where on earth is he? Why does he have to be so late? If people want to see people, they come when they say they will!

CONNIE: Easy, Lulu, easy.

LULU (*sobbing*): Oh, Connie, why did it have to happen to me so late? I can't lose it! I can't lose it! (*There is a knock. Lulu turns quickly toward the door, and her mood changes. She is fluttering with hope.*) Oh, maybe that's Paul. That must be Paul!

CONNIE: Go in and put your face on. (*Pushing Lulu gently toward the bedroom door*) And come out as if you'd never had a moment's worry about him. Go on.

When Lulu is out, Connie goes to the corridor door. She admits Paul.

PAUL: It's so good to see you, Connie. It's been much too long. (*He puts his hat and coat over a chair.*) Where's Lulu?

CONNIE: She's finishing dressing. She just got in a minute ago. Would you like a drink?

PAUL: I'll get it. May I fix you one?

CONNIE: I have one somewhere around. Oh, here. Yes, it has been a long time, hasn't it? But then I've seen hardly anything of Lulu either.

PAUL: You're such a busy lady. (*He is fixing himself a drink.*)

CONNIE: Oh, it's Lulu that's the busy one. Every time I tried to call her for the past week, she's been out.

PAUL: How is she? (*With his drink, he comes down toward the sofa.*)

CONNIE: Whatever she's been doing must agree with her. She looks wonderful.

PAUL (*picking up one of the two lending-library books on the coffee table*): Oh. She's been out a great deal?

CONNIE (*quickly*): Oh, those are mine. They're glorious. I read about beautiful young girls getting themselves chopped into pieces with an ax, and I think: I'm not doing so bad.

PAUL (*putting down the book*): Connie, I've missed you.

Lulu enters from the bedroom and comes quickly up to Paul.

LULU: Hello, darling. (*She kisses him on the cheek.*) Now why did you have to be so late? Where were you, anyway? I waited and waited.

CONNIE: Oh, God.

PAUL: I'm sorry.

CONNIE: Lulu Ames, you miserable fraud. Trying to put the blame on somebody else. Why don't you come clean and admit you're late, too? (*To Paul*) She just got in a minute ago.

LULU (*after a puzzled look at Connie*): Oh, Oh, dear, I had such pretty plans, and then I didn't get home in time. There was going to be entrance music and a blaze of light for you. Did you get my messages? It was nothing important. They were just to tell you not to hurry. I didn't want you to get here before I got back.

PAUL: I wanted to hurry but I couldn't. I had a cocktail party. It was a must. Don't you have those in the decorating business too, Connie?

CONNIE: Incessantly. Awful, aren't they?

LULU: You two. Where are your spines? I wouldn't do anything I didn't want to.

CONNIE: Lulu, stop talking about yourself and tell him about me.

LULU: Connie's firm is sending her abroad. Isn't that wonderful?

PAUL: That's fine. Congratulations. (*He shakes Connie's hand.*)

LULU: She asked me to go with her.

PAUL: She did? How long would you be gone?

LULU (*an edge coming into her voice*): You don't have to jump at it, Paul. I haven't said I'd go yet.

Connie, who is behind Paul, shakes her head warningly at Lulu.

CONNIE: But you did say you'd think about it.

LULU (*recovering*): Of course I'm thinking about it. I love to think about attractive things. That's how I got this creature on my mind in the first place. (*Patting Paul on the arm*) Forgive my being personal. And why don't you pour me a drink instead of standing there all the day idle?

PAUL: I'm sorry. (*He goes to fix Lulu a drink.*)

LULU: We'd be gone months and months, didn't you say, Connie?

CONNIE: At least.

PAUL: That's a long time to be away.

LULU: Go on twisting my arm, darling. I love it.

CONNIE: Well, the invitation still holds. (*She picks up her bag.*) I've got to go.

PAUL (*obviously disappointed*): Oh, aren't you going to have dinner with us?

CONNIE: I've got a million things to do.

PAUL: Let them all go. Stay where you're needed.

LULU: Paul, you heard her say she had to go.

CONNIE: I've got to wash everything I own. (*She holds out her hand.*) Good-by, Paul. When I get to Paris I'll send you a pretty postcard of the Guaranty Trust.

PAUL (*kisses her*): Good-by, Connie. All the luck.

She starts to go, Lulu going with her to the door.

CONNIE (*suddenly remembering*): Oh— (*She goes back, picks up the books from the coffee table.*)

LULU (*puzzled*): Connie, those aren't—

CONNIE (*quickly*): These are mine. (*She goes to the door; Lulu, still puzzled, follows her.*) You're a good girl, Lulu. A good, good girl. (*She goes. Lulu closes the door, turns back to Paul.*)

LULU: Good evening, Mr. Osgood.

PAUL: Good evening, Mrs. Ames.

LULU: You're looking unusually handsome.

PAUL: You're looking usually lovely. (*He kisses her on the cheek.*)

LULU: Don't let yourself go too far. No, I was only fooling. That was very nice indeed. (*Moving away from him*) Look at our table.

PAUL: I've been looking at it. It's charming.

LULU: I've developed quite a drag with the chef since you were here last. No menus tonight. It's going to be something rather special. What time is it, Paul?

PAUL: Twenty minutes to eight.

LULU (*lighting the candles*): Let's do this so they'll be the right height at dinner. Are you hungry?

PAUL: Famished.

LULU: Oh, dear. I told the chef eight o'clock. I don't dare ask him to hurry it up. Who would ask Michelangelo to hurry the Sistine Chapel? Now doesn't that look nice? Doesn't the whole room look nice?

PAUL: Yes, it does. And it feels nice too. It's like old times. (*He takes her hand.*)

LULU: The good old times, before the stormy weather started.

They look at each other for a moment, then kiss.

PAUL (*holding Lulu in his arms*): It's lovely and clear tonight.

LULU: It's going to stay that way. And that's not just a weather forecast; that's a promise.

They separate. Lulu takes her drink, sits on the sofa.

PAUL: Are you really considering going abroad with Connie?

LULU: Of course not. (*Paul gives her a quick look.*) Yes, I know what I said, but I'm finding out—and not for the first time, Mr. Osgood—how pleasant it can be here.

PAUL (*sitting beside her*): I'm afraid you'll miss her.

LULU: I don't seem to miss anybody but you. Still, I may. It's like the children. I really didn't want to see very much of them while they were here, but now they've gone away I feel ill used and bereft. Can you explain that?

PAUL: Easily. It's what's called human nature.

LULU: They love the country, and everything's fine. Oh, I knew I had something to tell you. Christopher patted a puppy the other day and didn't change color.

PAUL: So that's what all those parades were about.

LULU: Oh, this is so nice. Did you really want Connie to stay to dinner? Were you afraid to be alone with me?

PAUL: I was—a little.

LULU: Well, you're not now, are you?

PAUL: Look at me.

LULU (*after a pause, very casually*): Paul, who did you go to the cocktail party with?

PAUL: I went alone. I didn't stay long.

LULU: Who was there?

PAUL: Quantities of people. The Pasons, among others. They asked for you.

LULU: Did you tell them you were coming here?

PAUL: Why, no.

LULU: Oh, it wasn't anything you were proud of?

PAUL (*good-humoredly*): Rising winds and a sudden drop in temperature.

LULU: Nonsense. Continued clear. How's the shop?

PAUL: There's a new craze hit the town. It's called reading. The shop is jammed with people buying books. If there was a soda fountain you'd think it was a drugstore.

LULU: Look at me! (*She rises, goes to the record player, and puts on the de Falla music again.*) There's the blaze of light, but I forgot the music. Oh, and I nearly forgot something else. (*She takes the box from the chair, brings it to Paul.*) Here.

Paul rises, opens the box.

PAUL: Now what have you gone and done?

LULU: And don't tell me you've got one exactly like it, because you haven't.

PAUL ⎤ (*in unison; Paul meaning it, Lulu mocking him*):
LULU ⎦   Oh, Lulu, you shouldn't have!

Paul takes a dark blue dressing gown from the box; there is a white monogram on the breast pocket.

LULU: Do you like it?

PAUL: Of course I like it. It's a beauty. But my dear, sweet, idiot child, you gave me a dressing gown exactly three weeks ago.

LULU: You would have had this one sooner, but it took ten days to get it monogrammed. Aren't you going to put it on?

PAUL: Can't you give me a chance to admire it? I've never had two new dressing gowns at once. I didn't know anybody did. It's going to keep me awake all night deciding which one to wear.

LULU: Oh, no, you missed the idea. The other one is for you to have in your place. This one—this one is for you to keep here.

PAUL: Oh. (*He puts it back in the box.*) It's beautiful, Lulu. Thank you so much.

Lulu goes and turns off the music.

LULU: Why did you say "Oh" that way?

PAUL: Did I say it any particular way?

LULU: You know how you said it. Did you think I was too forward suggesting you keep a dressing gown here?

PAUL: Please, Lulu.

LULU: Because if you think it was an invitation—well, it was, I guess. That and a sort of welcome home. Paul, why have you been staying away? Is there somebody else?

PAUL: No.

LULU: Then why?

PAUL: Because of this, Lulu. These questions, these reproaches, this being made to feel guilty.

LULU: And why should you feel guilty?

PAUL: I guess because you want me to. There certainly isn't any other reason. But I have to watch everything I say for fear it will bring on a scene. Look, I can't say "Oh" without upsetting you.

LULU: No, and you can't deny what you meant by that "Oh."

PAUL: (*touching her arm*): Ah, Lulu.

LULU: Please don't touch me.

PAUL: You're right. That's no solution. (*He sighs.*) And this was going to be that nice clear evening.

LULU (*after a moment*): I'm sorry.

PAUL: I'm sorry too. (*He notices Sassy's plate on the mantel-*

piece.) Lulu, why do you keep little Sassy's plate up here? Ought you to do that?

LULU: Why not?

PAUL: Isn't it a little morbid?

LULU: That was her plate. I always washed it myself and put it up there so it couldn't get broken. Why is it morbid?

PAUL: To keep reminding yourself.

LULU: I didn't want to be reminded at first, but now I do. She was the only creature who ever loved me completely. Do you think I want to forget that?

PAUL: I guess not.

LULU: I'm never going to let the plate out of my sight. It's all I have.

PAUL: All right, Lulu. All right.

LULU: Morbid. Calling me morbid. Can't you understand anything?

PAUL: I said, all right. Let's stop this. Suppose you finish your drink. (*He hands her the drink.*)

LULU: I might as well. It seems to be the only thing that isn't finished.

PAUL: Come on. Tell me what you've been doing.

LULU: Waiting for you.

PAUL: Well, that didn't work very well, did it? (*Noticing the hat*) Oh, you've got a new hat. It's pretty.

LULU: I hate the sight of it. I'm going to give it to the Salvation Army.

PAUL: Very practical. Some wino will look great in it.

LULU: Paul, are you sure you went to that cocktail party alone?

PAUL: Here we go.

LULU: Have you heard from Sally?

PAUL: No.

LULU: Do you think she's coming back?

PAUL: I don't know.

LULU: If she does, I suppose you'll take her back like a shot?

PAUL: No.

LULU: But you'd sleep with her, wouldn't you?

PAUL: Lulu, we're now in the realm of pure fantasy.

LULU: Are you trying to tell me you've forgotten about her?

PAUL: No, I haven't. I don't suppose I ever will. The wound is healed, but the scar is there.

LULU: Well, I did a fairly good job, but I can't do plastic surgery.

PAUL (*with a great effort at remaining calm*): Lulu, what is it you want?

LULU: You. I guess that's too much to ask, isn't it? Skip me. What do you want?

PAUL: Not very much. Just to have some part in the world, and I know damn well how small mine is. I like my bookshop, and I'm glad that it does well. But I want to be among people. I don't mean just at cocktail parties and at dinner. All kinds of people. I want to know what they're thinking and what goes on. I guess I want to go on too. I don't want to be bricked up.

LULU: Don't you like me any more?

PAUL: I'm fond of you, Lulu; fonder than I've ever been of anybody. I'd give anything not to hurt you; I wish you well with all my heart; but this is all wrong.

LULU: Why?

PAUL: Because the sweetness has gone out of it—the loveliness.

LULU: Whose fault is that?

PAUL: I realize it can't just be one person's fault.

LULU: You realize that? Well, I realize it can be. It's yours. It was all sweet, it was all lovely when you'd see me every night. Paul, let's go away together—just us.

PAUL: We've been away together. Right here. Just us. And see what's happened to us. Face it, my dear.

LULU: I don't seem to be able to face anything now. It takes courage to face things, doesn't it?

PAUL: (*gently*): Yes, it does.

LULU: I guess I only had a spoonful of courage to begin with. And I used that up when I slammed the door of the house in Akron. I guess I'm like my name. I lack an heroic quality.

(*She gives a small laugh.*) People ought to be awfully careful what they name their children. . . . Paul, maybe I could change.

PAUL (*shaking his head*): People don't change, they just get more so.

LULU (*rising*): You're fine. You're all well, aren't you?

PAUL: I told you that.

LULU: And who did it for you?

PAUL: You did. We both know that.

LULU (*lashing out*): Then why can't you remember it? Why can't you be grateful?

PAUL: Is gratitude what you're asking?

LULU: Yes. Gratitude—pity—anything!

PAUL (*hitting the table*): Lulu, stop it! I can't see you degrade yourself like this!

LULU: You needn't ever see it again if you'd just come back! Oh, come back, Paul! Please come back!

PAUL: Lulu, please. (*He avoids her extended arms.*)

LULU (*mockingly*): Lulu, please! Lulu, please! A fine ending for a romance.

PAUL: It was a good, simple thing we had, Lulu, but you had to make it into a fairy tale with swoons and vows and bleeding hearts. You can't help it, because you have to sentimentalize everything.

LULU: When do I sentimentalize?

PAUL: Well, just a minute ago. About the little dog's plate. All that about the only creature that ever completely loved you. That isn't what it was. You meant it was the only creature for whom you didn't have to exert yourself. For God Almighty's sake, get yourself another dog and stop leaning on me!

LULU (*wild, hysterical*): You get out of here! You get out of here!

Lulu takes the plate, hurls it at Paul. It crashes on the floor in fragments.

PAUL (*with controlled rage*): You see, Lulu. You see.

He picks up his hat and coat, goes out. Lulu stands for a moment, looking after him. She makes no attempt to follow him; she realizes this is final. She looks at the smashed plate on the floor. She goes over to it, falls on her knees, and, sobbing, tries to fit the pieces together.

DARKNESS

ACT TWO

SCENE FIVE

Mildred Tynan's room. It is several weeks later, about midnight.

When the light comes up we discover Mildred in her nightgown, standing in front of the bureau mirror with a glass in her hand. A whisky bottle is on the bureau, and the playing cards are spread out on the card table.

MILDRED (*gay and high and talking to her image in the mirror*): What will we drink this one to? All right, to us again. Me here, and you there. (*She toasts herself.*) I wish we looked prettier, but we don't. All right, we were pretty once. What does it matter? It matters a lot, I guess. It matters you get old. I didn't mean to get old this way. I never had to look at you except to be told how pretty I was. And now here I am. I'm a mess, mess, mess, mess, mess, mess. Ya-ah! All right, so we don't look so good, but we're better off than we were when I'd look at you and see his face over my shoulder. (*Drinks.*) That was just fine, that was great! Oh, wasn't he handsome; wasn't he wonderful; oh, wasn't I a lucky girl that he married me! Yeah, sure! Sure it was fine! All that money. *Wheee!* All that money. I have to laugh now about the time I found out what he was. Dirty man! Dirty man! Ah, let's not talk about this any more. Let's have some fun, shall we? (*She raises her glass again.*) Come on. (*She starts singing "An-*

chors Aweigh" off key and raucously.) *I wish* I knew the words, but that doesn't matter. (*Again to the mirror*) You've stood by me, baby. Everything we got into. I never thought I'd see you here. (*She starts singing again. The telephone rings. She motions it to be quiet.*) Ah, shut up! Nobody wants to talk to you! What were we saying? "Anchors aweigh . . ." Ah, now they've spoiled it, it's no more fun. Hey, look, what are we going to do? (*The telephone stops ringing.*) I know what we're going to do. Nothing. There's nothing for us to do, nothing but this. Wretched little dark room. Have to phone down to find out what kind of day it is. We could get a room just as bad as this some place else, much cheaper. Sure we would have done it, but they won't let us out of here until the whole bill is paid. Don't like us here; well, we don't like them, so we're quits. That poor little nance, Mr. Humphries. Ah, he's not bad. He can't help it. Always asking me, asking me, asking me. It's not his fault. Did I say it was his fault? He's not mean. He kind of likes me. Irma likes me too. That's a friend and a half I got. Those old hags in the corridor. (*She raises her glass.*) Well, here's to them. There they are: money they've got—nothing to worry about they've got—twenty years of life they've got. And for what? Just to sit there. Vegetables they are, sitting there in their bins, waiting for the garbage collector to come and get them. So I get drunk and fall on my ear. Well, at least I'm not sitting down waiting. God, what would I be waiting for? Well, we got a little trouble here. I don't see much ahead, do you? Oh, dear, I wish you looked prettier. We used to look so nice. And look at us now. What am I? And God help me—what are you, standing there reminding me of myself? All right, all right, all right. But we used to look nice and we used to be nice. That thing I did with the bellhop. Think I feel good about that? I'm too nice for that. Whatever I am, I'm too nice for that. Yes, and I was too nice for that night I was coming home from the bars and the man came up behind me and knocked me out. I was too nice to wake up in that doorway, my head all bloody and my money gone. Think I want to go to the bars? Think they're any fun? Well, they're better than being alone, aren't they? Look at me, blind again. I'm stiff. All right, so I meant to be. If you can't understand that, we can't stick together much longer. (*The telephone rings.*) Excuse me. (*She goes to the telephone, takes it off the hook.*) There, that settles that. (*She turns away from the telephone, sees the cards spread out on the card table.*) To your wish, to your heart, to your house, to your hangover. Funny, I don't get hangovers any more. I've just got a running one that lasts all the time. (*She sweeps the cards off the table.*) Me that never drank until I found what he was really like. Once I got started—God, how he hurried me along. So when we went to the country club, Mrs. John Tynan would fall down on the dance floor and her husband would carry her out. And everybody would say, "Oh, that poor man, and look how sweet he is to her! Poor, dear man." Holy John Tynan, the Blessed Martyr of Santa Barbara. Yes, and the call girls, two and three at a time, and the whip in the closet. (*She makes a retching sound.*) Acgh. We weren't meant to be like this, were we? I guess it isn't what you're meant to be, it's what you turn out to be. All right, I think I'm pretty good. Look, I didn't always have to bore you, you. I had that little cat once, remember? I used to hold her up to look at you. Ah, so sweet. Gray, you know, mostly gray, but she sort of had her sleeves rolled up. (*She points a finger at herself in the mirror.*) It's a good thing, you know, to have a little animal in your room. If you talk to yourself, anybody passing by thinks you're talking to the animal. Ah, she was sweet, my kitty. Oh, well. (*She again starts singing "Anchors Aweigh," waving her glass wildly. There is a knock on the door.*) Wheeeee! We've got company! (*She goes to the door, opens it. Harry steps into the room, closes the door behind him.*) Oh. (*With *great dignity*) May I ask to what I owe this pleasure? Didn't you see that sign on the door?

HARRY: Hey, Mrs. Tynan, listen. It's pretty noisy in here.

MILDRED: And what affair is that of yours?

HARRY: They've been trying to telephone up from the desk. You took the telephone off.

MILDRED: And why shouldn't I? What have I got to say to them?

HARRY: They've got plenty to say to you. You're disturbing everybody on the corridor.

MILDRED: That's too bad. They're doing such important things.

HARRY: Yes, but they pay their bills. Why don't you? And why don't you put some clothes on?

MILDRED: I didn't expect company.

HARRY: Come on, pull yourself together, baby.

MILDRED: My name is Mrs. Tynan.

HARRY: All right, Mrs. Tynan. All I ask you to do is shut up. Because if you don't they're going to get an ambulance for you. Bellevue's waiting.

MILDRED: Why should there be an ambulance? I'm perfectly well.

HARRY: Yeah, you're great. You're in fine shape.

MILDRED: I certainly am. I've never felt better in my life.

HARRY: Sure, up here talking to yourself day and night.

MILDRED: Of course I talk to myself. I like a good speaker, and I appreciate an intelligent audience. (*Suddenly she giggles.*) I guess I read that somewhere, but it's me.

HARRY: All right, it's you. But I just tell you to shut up!

MILDRED: I'm sorry, but I don't take advice from bellhops.

HARRY: Oh, yeah? But you took a little more than advice from me once, didn't you?

MILDRED: Please go. I can't have this sort of thing.

HARRY: Oh, you can't! Who do you think you are anyway? Nothing but an old drunken bag, can't even pay her bill. Why don't you get wise? (*With the heel of his hand against*

her bare shoulder, he sends her spinning across the room.)
Why don't you take a running jump for yourself?

MILDRED: Funny, I never thought of that. It's an idea! Watch
me, bellhop! (*She rushes to the window, leaps out. Harry
stands stunned, then goes quickly toward the open window.*)

DARKNESS

ACT TWO

SCENE SIX

*The corridor. A November morning some months later.
Again the newspapers and the morning mail are in front of
each door.*

*When the lights come up Mrs. Lauterbach is opening her
door. She bends down, picks up a letter, begins to read it.
Mrs. Gordon appears in her wrapper.*

MRS. GORDON: See you got a letter. From your daughter?

MRS. LAUTERBACH: I was scared to open it. I thought
maybe they changed their plans and they weren't going to
have me up to Oswego for Thanksgiving. You know, like
last year. But this is just to tell me about trains. So everything's wonderful. My, I'm so excited I don't know what
I'm doing. I think I'd better take both my coats, don't
you? They don't have the Gulf Stream in Oswego, you
know.

*Charles Nichols opens his door; he is in shirt, trousers, and
slippers.*

MRS. GORDON: Morning, Charles. Did that sweet mother of
yours have a good night? (*Charles nods.*)

MRS. LAUTERBACH: You bring her down to the lobby this afternoon before you go out for your walk. I guess you'll be
hying yourself off to the zoo again.

CHARLES: Yes, I'll be hying myself off to the zoo again. (*He goes.*)

MRS. GORDON: I declare, he looks older than his mother does lately. (*She moves away from her door, looks in the direction of Lulu's room.*) Her Royal Highness must have got up early. Her paper isn't there.

MRS. LAUTERBACH: Maybe she's gone out again. A good thing for her to get out into the fresh air. She was an awful sick woman.

MRS. GORDON: You get mixed up with a young man, you're bound to be sick.

MRS. LAUTERBACH: Mrs. Gordon, have you noticed? She's letting her hair grow out to its own color.

MRS. GORDON: Best thing she could do. No sense trying to look young. Can't fool anybody.

MRS. LAUTERBACH: I'm glad she's better. I'm glad she gets out of her room.

MRS. GORDON: A lady starts staying in her room, after a while she gets so she never goes out of it.

MRS. LAUTERBACH: My, I was nervous while she had that "do not disturb" sign on her door. Those signs give me the creeps after what happened down the corridor. (*She motions toward Mildred's room.*) That was the way it was with Viola Hasbrook—that sign on the door—only hers was more of a natural death—not like that Mrs. Tynan, doing a thing like that.

MRS. GORDON: A terrible thing to have happen in a hotel. I almost thought I'd move out, except they kept it out of the papers. (*Irma enters with pail and mop.*) Good morning, Irma.

MRS. LAUTERBACH: Well, Irma, you brought us a nice day.

MRS. GORDON: You want to come in and do me now, Irma? You can start on the living room.

IRMA: All right, Mrs. Gordon, I'll be back. (*She goes out.*)

MRS. LAUTERBACH: I wonder if it still makes her feel funny, going into that room Mrs. Tynan had.

MRS. GORDON: That's a bad-luck room. Nobody stays there more than a week. I don't like the idea of transients. Don't know what kind of people you're getting.

MRS. LAUTERBACH: You know, I woke up the other night, and I could have sworn I heard her singing.

MRS. GORDON: Oh, stop it, Mrs. Lauterbach. You give me goose bumps all up and down.

MRS. LAUTERBACH: Certainly didn't envy Irma, having to go in there and get Mrs. Tynan's things together. She said there wasn't much. She said everything was all there, except she's still fussing about those missing cards. You know, that pack of cards she used to tell her fortune with. About half of them was gone, and they never turned up.

MRS. GORDON (*giggling*): Want to know a secret? I've been busting to tell you all this time. I took those cards.

MRS. LAUTERBACH: Virginia Gordon, you didn't!

MRS. GORDON: Oh, yes, before they locked up the room. I just said to myself, I'm going to have a few of these little old cards for a souvenir— Oh.

Lulu appears; she wears an autumn outfit.

MRS. LAUTERBACH: Good morrow, fair lady.

LULU: Good morrow.

MRS. GORDON: I see you're out bright and early. Makes us feel kind of lazy.

LULU: I have to go to the needlepoint shop. I want some more deep rose wool.

MRS. LAUTERBACH: You do a lot of needlepoint?

LULU: Oh, yes.

MRS. GORDON: Well, it fills up the time, I suppose. We were kind of wondering what you do with yourself all day long. We thought maybe you were getting ready to go back to Akron.

LULU: Oh, no.

MRS. LAUTERBACH: No, of course, Mrs. Gordon. She wouldn't want to go so far away from her children. When you've been sick, that's when you need your family.

LULU: My children don't live in New York, but my son comes to see me every Wednesday.

MRS. GORDON: Yes, I've noticed that. Just as regular.

LULU: Last week he brought me new photographs of my grandchildren. The baby girl is darling.

MRS. LAUTERBACH: You're going to spend Thanksgiving with them, I expect.

LULU: I don't know yet.

MRS. GORDON: We haven't been seeing much of you lately. Now that you're feeling better, why don't you come to the movies with us this afternoon? (*She holds Lulu by both arms.*)

LULU: Why, that's very sweet of you. (*She disengages herself.*) But I don't think I will, thank you.

MRS. GORDON: Now what are you going to do? Sit in your room and do your needlepoint?

LULU: Yes, I think so.

MRS. LAUTERBACH: Oh, you don't want to do that.

LULU: Yes, I really do, you know.

MRS. GORDON: Well, if that's what you want. But you can't do it forever.

LULU: Oh, I haven't made any plans about forever. I'm just trying a day at a time.

MRS. LAUTERBACH: It helps to make out a list of things to do—things to fill up the day.

LULU: I've been making up another kind of list—just in my head. A list of things I'm not going to do and things I'm not going to be. (*She turns to go.*)

MRS. LAUTERBACH: Well, if you ever want company, here we are.

MRS. GORDON: Mustn't let yourself get lonely.

LULU: Thank you, ladies. You're very kind. But there is really no need to worry about me. I'm quite all right. I'm not even

scared. You see, I've learned from looking around, there is
something worse than loneliness—and that's the fear of it.
I hope the movie is good. Good morrow. (*She goes. The
ladies look after her.*)

CURTAIN

Explanatory Notes

Scene One

3   *the East Sixties*   In Manhattan, an exclusive Upper East Side neighborhood.

3   *transient guests*   Short-term residents who pay by the night.

4   *Dresden china*   Fragile china, to be handled gently.

4   *hair . . . tinted gentian blue*   A certain type of rinse once favored by women with gray or white hair.

4   *small black hat . . . mink cape*   In the 1950s, a stylish ensemble popular with mature women who dressed expensively.

4   *lending-library book*   New titles made available by bookstores for customers wishing to borrow books at a small charge.

5   *"what's new on the Rialto?"*   A New York phrase, dating back to the 1880s, which inquired about what was going on in show business. Also an echo of a line from *The Merchant of Venice*, "What news on the Rialto?"

6   *"our third Musketeer"*   Three inseparable friends in Alexandre Dumas's novel *The Three Musketeers* (1844).

6   *the zoo*   Central Park Zoo, located at 64th Street and Fifth Avenue.

8   *broadtail*   A fragile coat made from the fur of a young lamb.

9   *"Mrs. Elliott Ames"*   An old-fashioned form of address, in which a married woman identified herself by her husband's given name.

9   *Akron, Ohio*   City of 200,000 located in northeastern Ohio, historically known as the home of the rubber industry.

Scene Two

14   *ormolu clock*   Imitation gold.

Scene Three

31   *Schrafft's*   A restaurant chain known for its genteel atmo-
     sphere and hot fudge sundaes.
32   *"She's a Jew"*   Casual anti-Semitism of the period.

Scene Five

44   *"Minute Waltz"*   "Waltz in D flat major" by Frederic
     Chopin.

Scene Six

48   *Columbia*   Columbia University located on Manhattan's Up-
     per West Side at Broadway and 116th Street.
48   *switchboard*   System of operator-assisted telephone calls,
     prior to the development of direct dial calls.

ACT TWO

Scene One

64   *"Anchors Aweigh"*   Official song of the U.S. Navy (1906).

Scene Four

84   *"El Amor Brujo"*   "Love the Magician," a piece for voices,
     actors, and orchestra composed by Manuel de Falla, 1914.

Scene Five

99   *poor little nance*   Homosexual man.
101 *Bellevue*   Bellevue Hospital Center, the oldest public hospital
     in the United States, known for psychiatric treatment. Lo-
     cated at First Avenue and East 27th Street.

Printed in the United States
by Baker & Taylor Publisher Services